PUPPY PATROL

HOMEWARD BOUND

JENNY DALE

Illustrations by Mick Reid
Cover illustration by Michael Rowe

AN
APPLE
PAPERBACK

SCHOLASTIC INC.
New York Toronto London Auckland Sydney
Mexico City New Delhi Hong Kong Buenos Aires

SPECIAL THANKS TO CHERITH BALDRY

No part of this publication may be reproduced, in whole or in part, or stored in a retrieval system, or transmitted in any form or by any means, electronic, mechanical, photocopying, recording, or otherwise, without written permission of the publisher. For information regarding permission, write to Macmillan Publishers Ltd., 20 New Wharf Rd., London N1 9RR Basingstoke and Oxford.

ISBN 0-439-45354-2

12 11 10 9 8 7 6 5 4 3   4 5 6 7 8/0

Printed in the U.S.A.   40
First Scholastic printing, July 2003

CHAPTER ONE

"Jake!" Neil Parker almost tripped over his excitable young Border collie as he bounded up, barking loudly. "Jake! *Down!*"

Jake still got excited easily, but he was learning to be obedient. He flopped down on the grass and looked up at Neil with bright eyes, his jaws parted in a doggy grin.

Neil peered around the side of the huge cardboard box he was carrying and grinned back at him. "I know, boy," he said. "It's just great to be here."

He gazed across the grass to the riverside and the barge that would take him and his family along the Norfolk River for a week's vacation. The sun was shining, and a warm summer breeze was blowing through his spiky brown hair.

1

Carole and Bob Parker, Neil's mom and dad, ran a boarding kennel and rescue center in the small country town of Compton. All of their friends called the Parker family the Puppy Patrol, because their lives were filled with dogs and they did so much for them.

It wasn't often that the Parkers could get away on vacation, but for the next few days, Neil's Uncle Jack would be keeping an eye on things at King Street Kennels, with the help of Kate and Bev, the Parkers' full-time kennel assistants.

Even though Neil loved life at the kennel, he was looking forward to his week off — just as long as there would be dogs to share it with him.

"OK, Jake," he said. "Let's move it. Heel!"

Staggering under the weight of the box, Neil headed toward the barge. It was a long, low boat, painted blue and white, with a cabin and a section of open deck at the stern. Its name was the *Wayfarer*.

When Neil reached the barge, he handed the box down to Carole Parker, who was standing on the deck with more boxes and bundles around her.

"What's in here?" he asked, flexing his aching arms. "It weighs a ton!"

"Food," Carole said. "I'll need more than a ton to feed you all — not to mention Jake!"

Jake, who had trotted obediently behind Neil, let out a sharp bark.

"OK, boy," Neil said, laughing and ruffling Jake's

black-and-white fur. "We haven't forgotten you! I packed all *your* favorite food myself."

Emily, Neil's ten-year-old sister, appeared from where their Range Rover was parked, with a bulging duffel bag in each hand. "I think that's everything," she said as she passed them down to her mom.

"Great," said Carole. "Then as soon as your dad's ready, we'll be on our way."

Bob Parker had gone into the boatyard with the owner of the barge, Mr. Hayden, to deal with the paperwork for their week's rental. While they waited for him, Carole started to put away their supplies. Neil watched Jake sniffing curiously around the deck.

"I can't wait!" Emily said. "Just think, in a couple of days we might actually meet Kerry Kirby again!"

Neil rolled his eyes. "Tell me about it!"

Emily was a big fan of the pop band All Spice, especially its singer, Kerry Kirby. Not long ago, the Parkers had looked after Kerry's dog, Molly, who was nearly as famous as her owner. Molly's fans had been a real pain. They had even invaded King Street Kennels during the night to get a glimpse of their favorite star's dog.

Emily elbowed Neil in the ribs. "You like her, too!"

"She's OK," said Neil, "but Molly's great!"

"Anyway," said Emily, "we wouldn't be here now if it wasn't for Kerry Kirby."

Neil shrugged. He wasn't going to admit it, but

Emily was right. The reason that their mom and dad had chosen this vacation was that All Spice was performing on the second day of an open-air festival organized by the SPCA. It was going to be held at Askham Bay, several miles downriver. Kerry Kirby had sent them the festival guide, along with backstage passes for the whole family. It seemed like too good an opportunity to miss.

Emily pulled the guide out of her jeans pocket. "Look," she said. "All Spice tops the bill. And there's Sugar Candy — that's the band that Dee Dee Drake formed when she left All Spice."

"*Sugar Candy?*" said Neil. "What sort of name is that?"

Emily sniffed. "Don't blame me. They probably stink, anyway."

Just then, Neil spotted Bob Parker coming out of the boatyard along with the barge's owner. Neil's five-year-old sister, Sarah, was jigging along beside her dad, holding his hand. Neil held on to Jake in case the lively young dog got in the way as they came aboard.

It seemed to take forever for Mr. Hayden to explain the workings of the *Wayfarer* to Bob and Carole, but at last he said good-bye and went back to shore. "OK — here we go!" said Bob as he started the engine and cautiously turned the wheel.

The engine chugged softly as the barge pulled

away from the bank. Sarah gave an excited squeal. "We're moving! We're moving!"

Neil leaned on the rail and watched as the river opened out in front of them. On one side was a row of houses; some of them had lawns that stretched down to the riverbank, while others were raised up over the water with a boathouse underneath.

"It would be great to live there!" said Emily. "You could go on the river every day."

"Maybe." Neil wasn't convinced. "It would be harder to keep dogs, though."

On the opposite side of the river, a reed bed stretched away as far as Neil could see. The feathery tops of the reeds swayed gently in the breeze. Emily

pointed out a wooden walkway that led away from the bank and disappeared among the reeds.

"That's for bird-watchers," she explained knowledgeably, "because the ground is so marshy. I read about it in my bird book."

"I can see birds," Sarah said, pointing to where some small black birds were paddling back and forth in the water beside the reed bed. "They're sweet."

"Moorhens," said Emily.

"I want to take one home," Sarah announced. "It can be a friend for Fudge."

Neil and Emily glanced at one another and groaned in chorus, while Carole tried to explain to Sarah why her hamster wouldn't want a moorhen for a friend.

Bob was still steering carefully. The river was busy with other boats — barges like their own, streamlined cruisers, and smaller fishing boats. A boat with a bright, blue sail glided across the river in front of them, and the man at the helm waved. Neil waved back happily. There was so much to look forward to — a whole week on the river, lots of sunshine and, best of all, Jake at his side and more dogs to meet when they got to the festival!

The river was becoming more and more crowded. Before long, Bob had to slow down to avoid hitting the boat in front.

"Why are there so many boats?" Sarah asked.

Carole was looking at the map. "There's a lock up ahead. Everybody must be waiting for the gates to open."

Sarah giggled. "There aren't gates on a river!"

"Wait and see," said Bob.

Peering along the line of boats in front of them, Neil could just see the lock gates. As he watched, they opened slowly, and more boats began to nose their way out into the river, heading upstream.

Their own line of boats began to move, and Bob had to maneuver the *Wayfarer* carefully between the gates and into the lock.

"Steady," Carole warned him. "Watch out for that —"

Too late. Bob cut his speed, but the barge was still moving forward. Neil winced as it collided with the motorboat just ahead. Fortunately, it was no more than a gentle bump. A shout of "Hey! Watch it!" came from the boat's driver.

"Sorry!" Bob called back. He was looking flustered and embarrassed.

"Captain Bob Parker, the terror of the seven seas," Neil said to Emily with a grin. With his curly brown hair and beard, his dad only needed an eye patch and a parrot to make him look exactly like a pirate. But he certainly wouldn't make a good pirate chief unless he learned to steer a lot better.

"Want me to take over?" Carole asked.

"Sure." Bob laughed as he let Carole take his place. "Dogs, I can cope with. Boats are a bit harder to handle."

Neil was impressed by how skillfully Carole edged the barge forward until it was close to the other set of gates at the far end of the lock. By now the lock was full of boats, and the gates were closing again behind them. Neil stared as the water level started to fall and the sides of the lock gradually became visible. It was weird looking up to the higher level where they had been sailing just a short time before.

At last, the lower gates opened. The crowd of boats quickly thinned out as they were able to move into the river again.

"Phew!" Bob mopped his brow with a huge handkerchief. "How many more of those do we have to go through?"

"None between here and Askham Bay," Carole said. "There aren't many locks on this river, because the land is mostly flat."

"Thank goodness for that!" said Bob.

In the excitement of negotiating the lock, Neil had forgotten to keep an eye on Jake. Now he looked around. There was no sign of the young Border collie on the forward deck.

"Hey, where's Jake?" Neil said, fighting against the urge to panic. If his dog had gone overboard while they were in the lock, he could have been crushed between the boats. "Jake! Jake!"

Swiftly, he worked his way along the narrow passage between the cabin and the side of the barge. Jake wasn't on the stern deck, either.

Emily was following. "He couldn't have gone far," she reassured Neil. "We would have seen him if he'd jumped in the river."

"Jake, where are you?" Neil called, beginning to panic.

To his relief, an answering bark came from the cabin. With Emily behind him, Neil climbed rapidly down into the narrow passage between the bunks, then through to the tiny galley.

"Maybe he's hungry," he said. "I wouldn't say no to a snack myself."

The galley was lined with built-in storage cupboards so that everything could be stowed away tidily. Jake was scraping at the door of the one underneath the sink.

"Come out!" Neil said. "There's nothing there."

Jake whined and went on scraping. The door was a sliding one, already partly open, but Jake couldn't open it any farther.

Neil suddenly froze as a whimpering noise came out of the dark space beyond.

"What was that?" he said urgently.

"Maybe it's a rat," said Emily.

Neil crouched down beside Jake and put a hand on his collar. "OK, boy," he said. "Let's have a look."

He pushed the sliding door back as far as it would go and gasped as he looked into the cupboard. Huddled inside it, huge eyes gazing up at him with an unhappy expression, was another dog.

CHAPTER TWO

"**S**he's only a pup," said Bob. He stroked the trembling dog with his big, gentle hands. "About six months old, I'd guess."

Neil had brought the stowaway dog up on deck, and Carole had steered the *Wayfarer* to the bank and cut the engine while everyone examined her. She was big, though obviously still young, as Bob had said. Her coat was a glowing golden color, long and slightly wavy, and Neil could imagine how it would shine when the pup was in good condition. She had white markings on her front and paws, and a white tip to her tail.

She whimpered anxiously as Bob touched her, but she didn't shrink away or try to bite him. She was nervous, but Neil could tell she wanted to trust him.

"I thought she was a Labrador at first," he said. "But she's not, is she?"

"No," said Bob. "Now let me get this right — she's a Nova Scotia duck tolling retriever."

"A *what*?" Emily asked. "I've never heard of a dog called that!"

"Toller for short," Bob explained. "They were bred to splash around in shallow water and flush out ducks so that hunters could shoot them."

"Horrible!" said Emily, stroking the toller's head and looking down into her gentle face. "You wouldn't do that, would you, girl?"

"I don't think so," said Bob. "But I bet she's a good swimmer." He picked up one of the pup's front paws and held it in the palm of his hand. "Look, webbed feet. And that dense coat is to keep her warm in the water."

Neil laughed. "She's really something! But I wonder what she was doing hiding on our boat."

The stowaway puppy was gradually calming down, and soon she managed to lap some water from the bowl Neil had filled for her.

"She must have come with us from the boatyard," said Emily. "Maybe she belongs to the owner."

"I doubt it," said Bob. "My guess is she's a stray, or she's been neglected. She doesn't look too bad, but she's very thin. I can feel her ribs."

"People shouldn't have dogs if they can't look after

them properly," Neil said indignantly. "She's not even wearing a collar."

He fished out a dog treat from the supply he always carried in his pocket and held it out in the palm of his hand to the strange dog. She sniffed at it cautiously, then crunched it up and looked for more.

"Good girl!" said Neil. He gave her another tidbit, and one to Jake, who came pushing in for his share. "I wish she could tell us her name," he added. "And where she comes from."

"Emily's right," said Carole. "She must have stowed away while the barge was moored at the boatyard. We'll have to take her back."

"But we'll miss the festival!" Emily protested.

"I want to keep her," said Sarah, stroking the toller's head. Sarah wanted to keep *every* dog they found.

"We can't do that," Carole said. "She's not ours. Bob, what do you think?"

"I'm not going back through that lock again," Bob said. "Especially since we don't know that we'd find her owner if we did." He reached inside his backpack for his cell phone and switched it on. "Just as I thought — I'm not getting any signal here. I think we should continue on to the festival for the time being. We can stop off when we see a pay phone and call the boatyard. If Mr. Hayden knows whose dog she is, we can make arrangements to hand her over."

"Not if her owner's neglecting her," Emily said determinedly.

Her dad nodded. "I'll do my best to make sure she'll be OK."

"And if we don't find her owner?" Carole asked.

"Then she can come home with us," said Bob. "To the *rescue center*," he added as Sarah gave a squeal of delight. "Don't worry. We'll make sure she gets a good home."

"One where she'll be properly looked after," said Neil. He patted their new friend. "Don't you worry, girl. You'll be OK with the Puppy Patrol!"

Before they set out again, Bob heated some soup and made sandwiches for lunch, while Neil fed the stowaway puppy. She wolfed down the mixture of meat and biscuits, and looked much perkier when she had finished. She settled down at the stern of the barge, gazing out over the water with bright, alert eyes. She looked as if she really belonged on the river.

Jake nosed up to the strange puppy, sniffed cautiously, then sat down beside her. Neil was glad that the two dogs had decided to become friends.

He kept an eye on them when the *Wayfarer* moved off again, and wondered about choosing a name for the toller. Emily was sitting beside him, deep in her bird book, trying to identify all the different kinds of birds that she saw.

"I'm going to keep a list," she said, "with the date I saw them, and — Neil, look, there's a heron!"

Neil turned his head in time to see a big, gray bird take off from the edge of the reeds and fly away with slow, strong wing-beats. At the same moment, there was a sharp bark from the stowaway puppy and a splash. Neil turned back and saw Jake with his paws on the side of the barge, peering down into the water.

"Dog overboard!" Neil yelled. "Mom, stop!"

He scrambled across the deck and looked down into the river. The toller was swimming strongly, paddling across the current. At first, Neil thought that she was trying to chase the heron. Then he saw that she was heading for a sailing dinghy that was sailing toward the *Wayfarer* from the opposite direction.

The *Wayfarer* slowed down. "What's going on?" asked Bob as he appeared from the forward deck.

"Look!" Neil pointed. "She's an amazing swimmer."

As he spoke, the puppy reached the dinghy. The helmsman, a young man in shorts, had already seen her and was steering toward her. The girl with him loosened the sail to cut their speed. Then she leaned over the side, reached down, and managed to grab the puppy and haul her on board. The puppy stood and shook herself, then jumped up at the girl, barking excitedly.

Meanwhile, Carole was maneuvering the *Wayfarer* closer to the dinghy, so that they could talk to the other crew without shouting.

The girl was grinning widely as she tried to calm the excited pup. "Down, Lucy! Sit!" The puppy obviously recognized her name and sat at once.

"Hi," Neil said as the dinghy came alongside. "Is this your dog?"

The girl looked puzzled. "No, she's not. Where did you find her? Wasn't she with Jim?"

"Who's Jim?" Neil asked.

"Lucy's owner," said the young man at the dinghy's helm. "He has a barge like yours — he uses it to take people on boat trips."

"Where can we find him?" Emily asked.

Bob explained how they had found Lucy stowed away on their barge. The girl laughed and rumpled

Lucy's ears. "You're a terror!" she said. "You're a real river dog! I bet Jim's missing you."

Neil was relieved that they seemed to think Jim cared about his pup. Maybe Lucy was only thin and hungry because she'd been lost. "So where does Jim live?" he asked.

"On his barge, as far as I know," the girl said. "It's called *Green Lady*. But come to think of it, I haven't seen it around for the last couple of weeks."

"That might be when Lucy went missing," Neil said. "It would explain the condition she's in. She hasn't been properly looked after and she was really scared when we found her."

The girl crouched down and ran her hands along Lucy's silky, golden coat. "She *is* thin!" she exclaimed. "You poor girl! What are we going to do with you?"

Lucy thumped her tail vigorously on the boards of the dinghy.

"She can come with us," Neil said quickly.

The two boats were close enough for Neil to lean over and scratch Lucy's ears. She turned her head and slurped her tongue over his hand, then hopped over the side and back on board the barge. Neil could see she was a really friendly puppy.

Bob looked thoughtful. "We can look after her for now," he said. "My name's Bob Parker. We're going downriver for the festival at Askham Bay. Will you tell Jim where we are if you see him?"

"Sure," said the young man.

The girl leaned over to give Lucy a farewell pat. "We'll ask around," she promised. "She's a great puppy — I hate to think of her in trouble."

"She's not in trouble now," Neil said. "We'll make sure she's OK."

That evening, the Parkers moored their barge on the edge of a small village halfway to Askham Bay. Bob went to find a phone to call Mr. Hayden, the boatyard owner, and ask if he knew anything about Lucy's owner Jim.

While he was away, Neil and Emily pitched their tent. They had decided to camp on the bank each night because the barge was a bit cramped for five people to sleep in.

"Hey, Jake," Neil said as the young Border collie grabbed one of the tent pegs. "That really isn't helping!"

Jake dropped the tent peg but, when Neil went to pick it up, he grabbed it again and darted off. Lucy followed him, and the two young dogs started chasing each other along the riverbank.

"Bring that back!" Neil yelled.

Laughing, he ran after the two dogs, and flung a stick into the river for Jake to fetch. The Border collie dropped the tent peg, but before he could jump in, Lucy was ahead of him, swimming strongly to where the stick bobbed in the current.

Neil stood watching for a minute, admiring Lucy's skill in the water. The girl in the dinghy had been right — she *was* a real river dog.

Jake let out a soft whine. Neil stooped to pat him. "OK, boy, I haven't forgotten you," he said. "Your turn next."

He took the stick from Lucy as she came scrambling up the bank to give it to him. As he threw it again for Jake, trying to avoid the shower of water that Lucy shook over him, he noticed a barge full of people drawing up to a landing dock a few yards farther downstream.

"Hey, Em!" he called. "Come and look at this!"

Emily left the tent and joined Neil on the bank. By now the barge was moored, and people were starting to get off. An elderly man said good-bye to them as they left.

"It looks like he's doing boat trips," Emily said. "Do you think he's Jim?"

"No. His barge isn't called *Green Lady*," said Neil. "But he might know Jim. Let's ask."

They waited for Jake to come back with the stick, panting and sleek from the water, then set off along the bank. Before they reached the man, Lucy gave a joyful bark and bounded ahead to meet him.

"Uh-oh," said Neil. "She's found another friend."

The barge man patted Lucy and looked up at Neil and Emily with a smile. "Hello, there," he said. "What can I do for you?"

"We're looking for Lucy's owner," Neil said. "We think his name's Jim."

"You're not Jim, are you?" Emily asked.

"No, my name's Matt," the barge man said. "Matt Sykes. I know Jim Carter, though. We're in the same line of work."

"Do you know where we can find him?" Neil asked.

Matt scratched his thinning white hair. "I'm not sure I do. He used to run trips in the *Green Lady*, but he sold her a couple of weeks ago."

Neil and Emily exchanged a dismayed look. If Jim Carter had sold his barge, their best clue to finding him was gone.

"Do you mean he moved away?" Emily asked.

"I think he did," said Matt, ruffling Lucy's golden fur. "He was always a restless guy. Said he was sick of the river and he wanted to better himself. He told me he got a job with a band up in London."

"A band!" Emily exclaimed. "Which band?"

Matt shook his head. "I couldn't say. It sounded like a crazy idea to me."

"Then if he's gone to London," Neil said, "he must have left Lucy behind!"

He was starting to feel angry again at the thought that Jim really had abandoned his dog. He couldn't understand how anybody could do that, especially to such a friendly pup.

"Well, she was a stray," Matt explained. "I don't know where she came from to begin with, but I saw her a few times, up and down the river, before Jim took her on. Maybe he left her, maybe he handed her over to somebody else."

"We found her hiding on our barge," said Neil. "We *were* trying to track Jim down, but if she's a stray . . ." He trailed off, uncertain now.

"I'm sorry I can't be of more help," Matt said. "She's a good dog — she deserves a good home." He gave Lucy a farewell pat.

As Neil and Emily walked back to the tent with both dogs at their heels, Neil wondered what they should do next. It looked as if Jim Carter didn't want Lucy anymore, but they couldn't really find her another owner unless they were sure. They still needed to talk to Jim.

"I think we should try asking around at the festival," said Neil thoughtfully. "There'll be lots of local people there, and someone's bound to know where Jim is."

"He might even be there himself if he's in a band," suggested Emily. "There'll be tons of bands there."

"Yes! It's definitely worth a try," said Neil. "And if he is, we'll find him. I've got a few words to say to Mr. Jim Carter if we ever catch up with him."

CHAPTER THREE

The morning mist still lay heavily on the river as Bob Parker steered the *Wayfarer* into Askham Bay. The third day of their vacation was just beginning. Although Lucy had met several more friends on their journey downriver, they hadn't discovered anything more about the missing Jim. Finding him at the festival seemed like their last hope.

Several boats were already moored along the banks of the bay, and tents were pitched on the grass. Beyond that, Neil could just make out the entrance gate to the festival grounds, topped by a huge banner.

Carole had booked a mooring in advance. It seemed to take forever to find their space and then to maneuver the barge into it. Neil was impatient to set off on his search for Jim.

"The festival doesn't open until midmorning," Carole reminded him.

"But we've got backstage passes," Neil said.

"And it'll be easier to find out if Jim is there before it gets really crowded," Emily added.

"OK," Bob said from the bank where he was fastening the mooring rope. "You two go ahead with Jake and Lucy. We'll meet you at lunchtime in the SPCA tent. Don't forget."

"I want to go with Lucy, too," Sarah said.

"No, Squirt," Neil said. "You'll only get in the way."

Sarah stamped her foot and looked sulky. Neil and Emily left their mom trying to persuade Sarah that it would be much more fun to stay on board the *Wayfarer* and feed the ducks.

The festival grounds were in a huge meadow that stretched down to the waterside. There was a temporary fence where eager fans were already gathering, hoping to catch a glimpse of their favorite stars.

Neil and Emily showed their passes to the man at the gate, who waved them through. Jake and Lucy trotted after them. Neil had put Jake on his leash, in case his adventurous doggy friend decided to investigate some of the electrical equipment. He didn't have a leash for Lucy, but she seemed content to trot along beside Jake and look around with bright, interested eyes.

"OK, girl?" Neil said. "You'll help us find Jim, won't you?"

Lucy let out a bark, as if she agreed. Neil remembered how she had gone to say hello to all her friends along the river. There was a good chance she would lead them to Jim, if he was on the site.

Around the edges of the festival grounds people were setting up booths, some of them to sell refreshments or crafts, others advertising various groups that cared for animals. Farther along was a huge tent with the SPCA sign outside it.

In the center of the grounds was the main stage, with a group of TV broadcast vans parked nearby. Stage lights and amplifiers had already been set up, and technicians were checking the equipment. One man stood at the front of the stage with a microphone, and his voice boomed out over the loudspeakers. "Testing . . . one, two, three. . . ."

When she heard the voice, Lucy gave a delighted bark and shot off toward the stage.

"Hey!" Neil said.

"It looks like Lucy's got another friend!" laughed Emily. "Maybe he'll know where Jim is."

They both gave chase. Lucy scrambled up the steps that led onto the stage and stood in front of the sound technician, wagging her tail hard.

"Hi," gasped Neil, rushing up after her and looking up from the ground below the stage. "Do you know where Jim is?"

The sound technician looked puzzled. "Who's Jim?" he asked. "And who's this gorgeous pup?"

"I thought Lucy knew you," Neil said, disappointed. "She's Jim's dog."

The technician laughed. "Maybe she just likes the loudspeakers," he said. He bent down and held the microphone for Lucy. "Say hi, Lucy."

Lucy barked, and the sound carried all over the festival grounds.

Emily giggled. "She's going to be a star!"

Lucy gave the microphone a good sniff, then trotted to the front of the stage as if she was going to launch into her opening number. A few people had stopped to watch.

"That's enough, girl," Neil said. Showing off was all fine and well, but it didn't help with finding Lucy's owner. He slapped his leg. "Here!"

Lucy took no notice. To his embarrassment, Neil had to climb up onto the stage and haul her off. One or two of the onlookers gave the puppy a round of applause.

When he got back to Emily and Jake, he saw that his sister was looking puzzled.

"What's the matter?" he asked.

"There was a man here, giving us a funny look," said Emily.

"They're all giving us funny looks!" Neil groaned. "It's this starstruck dog's fault!"

"No, I mean he was really *staring*. He. . . ." She swung around, scanning the people nearby. "He's gone now."

"What did he look like?" Neil asked.

"Small, thin . . . and a bit suspicious."

Neil shrugged. "Maybe he just doesn't like dogs," he said.

"Maybe." Emily didn't sound convinced.

While they had been talking, people had begun to flood through the gates toward the main stage. Neil realized that it was time for the festival to open. Just then, the crowd roared and Emily grabbed his arm. Her face had turned pink and her eyes were wide.

"Neil, it's Kerry Kirby!"

Neil swung around to see that the roadies had gone and the lead singer of All Spice was standing center stage. Her hair was different every time Neil saw her. Today, it was golden-brown and hung in twisty curls all around her face. She wore a white miniskirt and a white halter-neck top. Beside her, on the end of a jewel-studded leash, was her dog, Molly.

Neil was a lot more interested in Molly than he was in Kerry Kirby. She was a terrier crossbreed, with bright eyes and an appealing face. Her shaggy coat was the same golden-brown as Kerry's hair. Neil wondered if Kerry had dyed her hair to match her dog.

Molly sat happily at Kerry's feet while the pop star spoke to the crowd that had rushed to gather

around the stage. The TV reporters were filming, and photographers took pictures of the famous pair.

"Hi there, everyone!" Kerry said with a huge smile. "Welcome to the festival. Remember that we're doing this for the SPCA, so check out their tent and find out all about the kind of work they do. In the meantime, we've got some terrific bands for you, and I know you're all going to have fun. Let's go!"

In the applause that followed, Lucy wriggled through to the stage, put her paws up against it, and barked. Molly trotted forward and looked down at her over the edge. Then she barked in reply.

"Look at those two!" Emily said. "I think they want to be friends."

Kerry had come down from the stage and was singing autographs in books that her fans thrust at her. After a few minutes, she managed to make her way over to Neil and Emily.

"Hi there," she said. "Great to see you. Hey, that can't be Jake! Hasn't he grown?"

"Sure has," said Neil proudly. Jake had been a young pup when Kerry Kirby brought Molly to stay at King Street. "Molly looks good."

"Molly's great!" said Kerry.

She lifted her dog down from the stage, unclipped her leash, and placed her in front of Jake. The two dogs sniffed at each other, and Jake let out a joyful bark. He threw himself at Molly, and they rolled over together playfully.

"They haven't forgotten each other!" Neil said.

Not to be left out, Lucy let out a flurry of excited yaps and danced around the other two dogs, eager to join in.

"Wow, what a gorgeous puppy!" Kerry exclaimed. "What's her name?"

"Lucy," said Neil. "She's lost, and we're trying to find her owner."

"He must be worried sick, wherever he is," said Kerry. "She's a fantastic dog. Just look at her with Molly!"

The big toller puppy had flopped onto the grass with her paws in the air, and Molly flung herself on top. Neil couldn't help thinking that the two dogs looked as if they belonged together. They were almost the same golden-brown color, for one thing. Lucy was bigger, even though she was younger, but she was too gentle to hurt Molly in their game.

"They get along so well together!" Kerry said, laughing. "Neil, I've got to go and rehearse. You and Emily wouldn't look after Molly for me, would you?"

"Sure we would," said Neil. "All part of the Puppy Patrol service."

"Great," said Kerry, "If you —"

She was interrupted by a loud voice speaking just behind Neil. "I told you, *no*! Kerry's not giving interviews."

Neil turned to see Rachel James, Kerry's personal assistant, standing with her hands on her hips and glaring at one of the photographers. She was a tall, slim woman with red hair, and just now she looked furious.

"Oh, come on," the photographer was saying. "What about the rumor that —"

"Can't you understand plain English?" Rachel snapped. "No means *no*. Kerry has work to do."

Kerry walked over to Rachel and put a hand on her arm. "Hey, Rachel, cool it." Then she turned to the photographer. "Sorry, I've got to rehearse. Come to the photo shoot tomorrow."

The photographer raised her camera and fired off a couple of shots. She was a young woman, with cropped dark hair, dressed in jeans and a leather jacket. "And how about one with the mutt, Kerry?" she said.

"Molly is *not* a mutt," said Kerry. "And she'll be at the photo shoot, too."

The photographer still tried aiming her camera at Molly, but the terrier was dancing around Jake, pretending to bite his tail.

"Kerry," the photographer said, giving up on Molly, "the word is that you and Michael Newman are getting married soon."

"Listen, you rude woman —" Rachel began.

"Who are you calling rude?" the photographer demanded, suddenly starting to sound aggressive. "Kerry's news. Big news. My readers want to know everything about her."

"And you'll get it all at the photo shoot," Kerry said firmly. "Right now I have to work."

"So go *away*," said Rachel.

The photographer scowled at her, snapped one last picture, and shouldered her way into the crowds.

Rachel stared after her. "I've got a good mind to call her editor."

"Rachel, I said cool it," Kerry told her. "We need publicity, don't we? They're bound to get pushy — it's their job."

Rachel still looked angry. Neil wondered what her problem was. As Kerry's personal assistant, she must have dealt with hundreds of photographers. What was it about this one that was getting her so worked up?

"All right," she said, obviously making an effort to control her anger. "Where's Molly? I'll keep an eye on her while you're rehearsing."

"No need," said Kerry. "Neil and Emily here are going to look after Molly."

To Neil's surprise, Rachel flared up again. "But that's *my* job!"

Kerry looked just as surprised as Neil felt. "But they can help you, can't they? I thought you'd be happy. You've got lots of other things to do, and they're good with dogs."

"Molly's not just any dog," Rachel retorted. "She's Kerry Kirby's dog. Do you really think she'll be safe with a couple of kids?"

Neil exchanged a glance with Emily. She looked astonished, too. When Rachel had arranged for Molly to stay at King Street Kennels, she had been super-efficient and in control of everything. Now she was really losing it.

"That's just the point," said Kerry. "People know you're my assistant, so if they see Molly with you they'll recognize her immediately. She won't stand out nearly as much if she's with Neil and Emily." She hesitated, and then added, "I can't help worrying about kidnappers."

"Kidnappers?" Rachel sounded startled.

"Molly's so popular, I'm scared somebody might try to steal her. Everyone knows I'd pay anything to get her back — and there are so many people and distractions here at the festival, it could be the perfect opportunity for a thief —"

"Then let me look after her *properly!*" Rachel snapped.

"Listen, Rachel," Kerry said kindly, "I know you're overworked. You've done a fantastic job setting up this gig. Let Neil and Emily give you a hand."

"We'll enjoy it, no problem," Neil said.

"We'll take really good care of her," added Emily.

Rachel made another effort to calm down. "I was going to take Molly back to my trailer, and give her food and water. She could take a nap while I sort out your fan mail."

Kerry's eyes twinkled as she glanced at Molly, who was still playing with Jake and Lucy. "She doesn't look sleepy to me. She's having a great time with her friends and she needs exercise. I don't want her shut up in a trailer today. She — Hi there. What can I do for you?"

The last few words were spoken to a couple of girls who had come up with autograph books in their hands. Neil thought they looked about Emily's age. They were twins, small with blond hair pulled back in ponytails. Both of them wore All Spice T-shirts.

"Can we have your autograph, please, Kerry?" one of them said, coming up to the pop star while her sister hung back shyly.

"Not *now*," Rachel said irritably.

"Sure." Ignoring Rachel, Kerry took the books, signed her name, and handed them back. "Have fun!"

"Thank you." The other twin crouched down to pet Molly, who had taken a break in her game to lie panting on the grass. "We really love Molly. We think she's the best dog in the world."

"I think she's great, too," said Kerry with a smile.

"Kerry, you're already late," Rachel said urgently. "Let me take Molly."

She moved toward Molly as if she was going to pick her up, but the two girls were in her way.

Neil stepped forward. "She'll be fine with us —" he started to say. But Molly drowned out his words with a sudden spate of loud barking. Molly sprang to her feet, staring at something in the crowds around the stage. Startled, the two fans drew back.

Before Neil could reach her, Molly shot off. Still

barking, she dashed away from the stage. Scraps of turf sprayed from her paws as she changed direction to avoid a couple of onlookers. Seconds later, she had vanished into the crowd.

CHAPTER FOUR

"**H**ey, Molly!" Neil yelled. "Stop!"

As he sprinted toward the spot where Molly had disappeared, Jake and Lucy added their barking to his shouts.

"Em, hang on to them!" Neil called.

He didn't look back to see whether Emily was holding Jake and Lucy. He was too intent on catching Molly. He could still hear her barking, but as he paused to look around, the barks changed to a loud whining.

Pushing through the crowd toward the sound, Neil suddenly caught sight of her. She was in the arms of a tall, dark-haired man in jeans and an open-necked shirt. He wore dark glasses that made him look really sinister.

"Put her down!" Neil shouted, dodging a group of kids and nearly tripping over the leash of some-body's corgi. The stranger might be trying to steal Molly! Kerry had said that she was worried about kidnappers.

Molly was still whining and wriggling in the man's arms as if she was trying to escape. But just as Neil came panting up, he saw the terrier push her face up to the kidnapper's and start licking him vigorously. Molly was happy! Her joyful greeting knocked off the man's dark glasses. Neil stood openmouthed as he recognized Michael Newman, the English soccer star who was Kerry Kirby's boyfriend.

"Michael!" Kerry was laughing as she caught up with them. She held out her arms to take Molly. "I thought you wanted to stay away from the press?"

"I did, but Molly blew my cover," Michael handed Molly over and bent down to retrieve his dark glasses. "I guess it's too late now."

Already an excited crowd was starting to gather. Michael shrugged and began signing autograph books, but when one fan asked him whether it was true that he was going to marry Kerry, he just laughed and didn't answer.

"OK," Kerry said when the last book was signed. "I've really got to rehearse now. Neil, are you and Emily still OK with looking after Molly?"

"You bet!" said Neil.

"But I said I'd take her!" Rachel protested.

"No, Rachel." Kerry clipped Molly's leash onto her collar again and handed it to Neil. "You've already got way too much to do. I can't expect you to cope with everything. I'll see you after the rehearsal, OK?"

Rachel, tight-lipped, looked from her employer to Neil, and back again. Then, without a word, she spun around and marched off into the crowd.

"What's wrong with her?" Michael asked.

"Oh, she's uptight about this gig," said Kerry. "She'll get over it. Come on."

She tucked her arm through Michael's and led him away.

"When do you want Molly back?" Neil called after her.

"Can you manage for a couple of hours?" Kerry glanced over her shoulder. "I'll send Rachel to find you, OK?"

"OK," said Neil. He bent down to pat Molly, and fished out a treat for her. As Emily joined him, with Lucy and Jake, he noticed that she was frowning.

"What's the matter? Too many dogs for you?" he joked.

Emily's frown vanished into a grin. "No, but while everybody was crowding around Michael, I saw that shifty-looking guy staring at us again — the one I told you about."

"Maybe he's a soccer fan," Neil suggested absent-mindedly.

"Well, maybe . . . But when he saw me looking at him, he took off again." Emily paused, then, suddenly sounding more determined, she added, "I'm sure there's something funny about him and I want to know what it is."

By now the festival was in full swing. A steady stream of people was still pouring through the gate. Lots of them had brought their dogs. Some clustered by the various booths, or drifted in and out of the SPCA tent. Others crowded around the stage, where the first band was in the middle of their set. Lively music burst out of the loudspeakers.

"Let's check out the booths," Emily suggested. "I want to buy presents for Kate and Bev."

"OK," said Neil. "And maybe we can get something to eat. I'm starving!"

They headed off toward the edge of the festival grounds with the three dogs following. Neil was amazed at the attention that Molly was getting. Several people recognized the famous dog, and a lot of them came up to pat her. The twins in the All Spice T-shirts who had spoken to Kerry by the stage were now hovering nearby, watching Molly with adoring looks. Neil wished they would either come and talk to her or go away.

Lucy got her share of patting and stroking, too. She sat beside Molly and looked up at the terrier's fans with big, appealing eyes. Not many people could resist her. Neil asked himself yet again how Jim could bear to abandon her.

He and Emily lined up to buy ice cream from a truck, and Neil stood eating his while Emily looked at a booth that was selling pens and key rings with pictures of animals on them. Jake sat at Neil's feet and gazed up at him with his tongue hanging out as if he was hoping some ice cream might come his way.

"Not a chance," Neil said. "Hang on a minute and we'll go find you a drink. You, too, Lucy —"

He broke off as he felt a tug on Molly's leash. Turning, he saw that she was heading toward a young woman who was crouched down, holding out a piece of chocolate on the palm of her hand. Neil recognized the photographer who had hassled Kerry earlier that morning.

"Hey!" he said. "Molly — sit!" He twitched Molly's leash, but the little dog was too intent on the chocolate. Neil had to pull her away more firmly. "Don't do that," he said to the photographer. "Chocolate is bad for dogs."

"One piece won't hurt," the photographer said. "Here, girl."

She held the chocolate out again, but Neil kept Molly close beside him. "You're only doing it to get a picture," he said. "Kerry Kirby told you to wait for the photo shoot."

"Interfering kid," the photographer muttered.

Just then, Lucy trotted up and pushed her nose into the photographer's hand. The photographer tried to snatch the chocolate away from the puppy, slipped on the grass, and sat down hard, only just managing to save her expensive camera. The piece of chocolate went flying, and Lucy snapped it up.

Neil tried not to laugh. "Smart move, Lucy!" he exclaimed. He swallowed the last of his ice cream and bent down to give Molly a pat. "Come on, Molly," he said. "Let's go and find Em."

"Just a minute." The photographer struggled to her feet and took out her wallet. "Look . . . what would you say to a fiver? For just a couple of shots of the dog?"

Neil gaped at her. "What do you think I am?" he said indignantly. "I'm looking after Molly!"

"Oh, come on! You'll have her back before you know it!" The photographer thrust the money at Neil and tried to grab Molly's leash. Neil dropped Jake's leash as he struggled to pull Molly out of the young woman's reach. Jake darted forward, barking furiously at the photographer.

The photographer stepped back, suddenly looking anxious. "Call him off!"

Neil started to laugh. He knew that Jake wouldn't hurt anyone, but the photographer didn't. She looked even more worried when Lucy and Molly joined in the barking.

"These dogs are dangerous!" she blustered. "You're not fit to be in charge of them."

"Oh, yes, he is!" Emily had come up behind Neil and jumped to his defense. "You're the one who's upsetting them. Go away!"

The photographer was already backing off. "I'm going! You're all crazy!"

She headed quickly across the field and was lost among the crowds.

Applause suddenly broke out, and Neil realized that he and Emily were at the center of an amused group of bystanders. Embarrassed, Neil looked around for a way to retreat quickly. The argument with the photographer had attracted much too much attention to Molly, just when he and Emily were supposed to make sure she kept a low profile.

Then Emily grabbed his arm. "Look — he's there! In the green T-shirt!"

Neil looked in the direction she was pointing and saw a small, thin man with dark hair straggling over his forehead. His T-shirt and jeans looked dirty, and he could have used a shave. He seemed to be staring straight at Neil and Emily, but almost as soon as Neil looked up, he quickly turned away.

"Who's he? And why was he staring at us like that?" said Neil.

"It's that weird guy I told you about," said Emily. "I keep seeing him, and he always seems to be giving us strange looks. I think he might be following us."

"OK, we'll ask him," Neil said. But as soon as he took a couple of steps in his direction, the man turned away. By the time Neil had managed to get through the circle of onlookers, he had disappeared.

"Weird or what?" said Emily, joining her brother. "That's three times now I've seen him." She ticked them off on her fingers. "By the stage, then near Michael Newman, and just now."

Neil looked thoughtful. "Maybe it's not us he's following. . . ." He gripped the end of Molly's leash even tighter and looked down at the shaggy little dog. "Maybe he wants to steal Molly."

* * *

Even after his ice cream, Neil's stomach was telling
him that it was lunchtime. He and Emily started to
make their way across the festival grounds toward
the SPCA tent where they were meeting their parents.

"We haven't done anything about finding Lucy's
owner yet," Emily said.

"We don't even know that Jim's here," Neil reminded her.

"I know, but we should start asking some of the local people, like the booth holders, if they know anything about him."

"You're right," Neil agreed. All the excitement with
Molly hadn't made him forget how important it was
to track down Lucy's owner. "We'll give it a try, but
after we've eaten. The dogs need a drink, too. We can
take them back to the barge."

"Not for long, though," said Emily. "If Rachel comes
looking for us and can't find us, she's going to get *seriously* annoyed!" Just as Emily mentioned the personal assistant, they almost cannoned into her. She
was standing with her back to them, near the television broadcast van.

Neil halted abruptly. "We've got her for a couple of
hours according to Kerry. Rachel can't be looking for
us already!"

But he soon realized that Rachel wasn't interested
in them at all. She stood facing someone else — a

small, slim girl with very short hair dyed an electric shade of blue. She wore shorts and a top in the same bright color, and big platform shoes. She had a bad-tempered look on her face.

"You don't know what you're talking about!" she snapped at Rachel.

"Uh-oh!" Neil said softly.

With Emily's help, he gathered the dogs together and retreated into the shelter of the van. It was obvious that the two women didn't want to be overheard. Neil was about to slip away and leave them to their argument, but Emily gripped his arm and hissed into his ear, "That's Dee Dee Drake!"

"What? Who's she?" Neil asked.

"I *told* you. She used to be in All Spice, but she had a falling out with Kerry and left. She formed her own band — Sugar Candy — but they're absolute garbage!" She peered around the corner of the van.

Neil heard Rachel saying, "You don't pay my salary, so don't order me around."

Emily drew back again, puzzled. "I wouldn't have thought Rachel would want anything to do with Dee Dee after what she did to Kerry," she said. "So why is she talking to her now?"

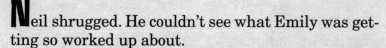

CHAPTER FIVE

Neil shrugged. He couldn't see what Emily was getting so worked up about.

He still wanted to leave before Rachel spotted them, but Emily whispered, "I want to find out what's going on."

She edged around the corner of the van. Neil didn't have much choice but to follow her, just in time to see Rachel break off her confrontation with Dee Dee. She strode away, past Neil and Emily, glaring at them but not speaking.

Neil and Emily were left facing Dee Dee.

"Huh!" she said. "So you've got Kerry's flea-ridden mutt!"

"Molly is *not* flea-ridden!" Neil replied. "She's very well cared for."

"She's a publicity stunt," Dee Dee said. "Kerry's got to get into the papers somehow, and it won't be for her singing, that's for sure."

"Kerry's a fantastic singer," said Emily.

"Oh, sure," Dee Dee sneered. "Just about as good as Molly!"

She took a few steps across the grass toward them, and Neil moved in front of Molly defensively. Lucy barked, as if she wanted to protect Molly, too.

"Wait till Sugar Candy gets going," Dee Dee said. "Then you'll see what a real band's like. And we don't need any stupid dogs, either!"

She stuck her nose in the air and strutted off.

"Good thing — for the dogs!" Emily called after her. Emily's face was pink, and her eyes were bright with indignation. "She's horrible," she said to Neil.

Neil crouched down and rubbed his hands through Molly's shaggy brown fur. Molly wagged her tail delightedly and put her paws up on his knees to lick his face.

"Don't you listen to her!" Neil said. "You're a great dog, Molly."

Jake gave a protesting bark.

Neil laughed. "Yes, so are you!" he said reaching out to ruffle Jake's ears. "And you, too, Lucy," he added as the toller puppy pushed in for her share of stroking. "You're all great!"

He passed out dog treats all around, and then got to his feet. "Come on — food!"

Jake stood alertly, wagging his tail, but Molly and Lucy were too busy rolling over together to take any notice.

"They really like each other!" said Emily. "They just want to be together all the time."

"That's nice to know," said Neil, grinning as he hauled on Molly's leash. "But I want my lunch!"

He managed to persuade Molly to walk alongside Jake. They set off again for the SPCA tent, with Lucy trotting after Molly as if she couldn't bear to leave her side.

"You know, Em," he said. "That gives me an idea."

"What about?"

"Molly and Lucy. They're getting along so well together. And when Molly boarded with us, I told Kerry that she'd be happier if she had a friend to play with. Remember?"

Emily's face split into a wide smile. "You think that Kerry should take Lucy? Neil, that's a brilliant idea! Molly's such a friendly dog — she must get lonely when Kerry can't be with her. And Lucy just loved being onstage!"

"Exactly," said Neil. "But we'll still have to find Jim somehow — or at least try. And then, if he really doesn't want Lucy, I'm going to ask Kerry what she thinks."

The SPCA tent had a display of photographs mounted on screens, and an information table with leaflets. Dogs and other animals were there, looked after by SPCA officers. Neil saw a long mesh pen with two or three rabbits hopping about playfully, and a vivid red-and-green parrot on a perch.

When Neil and Emily arrived, they saw that their parents and Sarah were already inside the tent. Bob was at the far side, chatting to one of the SPCA officers, while Carole and Sarah looked at the displays.

"Hi there," Bob said as Neil and Emily led the dogs over to him. "I see you've got the most famous pooch in the world again!"

"We're looking after her for Kerry Kirby," Emily said proudly.

"And what about Lucy?" Bob asked. "Any luck with her?"

Neil shook his head. "We're going to have a really good look for Jim just as soon as we've eaten."

"First things first!" said Bob, grinning.

Just then, Sarah came over to Neil and started tugging at his hand. "Neil! Come and look at this poor dog!"

She led Neil over to the nearest display board, where Carole Parker was looking at pictures of a dog the SPCA had rescued. He could hardly believe what he saw. The dog in the picture was painfully thin, with a coat so matted with dirt that Neil couldn't even tell what breed it was. One eye was closed, and the other gazed mournfully up at the camera.

Neil felt sick. He clenched his fists as a hot anger swept through him. He couldn't understand how anyone could mistreat a dog until it looked like the one in the picture. He had to glance down to reassure himself that Jake was there beside him, with his glossy coat and alert look.

"That's just awful!" said Emily, coming up beside Neil to gaze at the picture.

"But the dog was rescued," Carole said. "He's fine now."

"Do you want to meet him?" a voice said to Neil.

Neil turned around to see the SPCA officer who had been talking to Bob. He was a tall, gray-haired man with a thin, weather-beaten face. He smiled at Neil and Emily.

"You mean the dog is here?" Neil asked.

"He certainly is. Come and meet Nicky."

The officer led the way to a dog basket just behind the display screens. A black-and-tan Airedale terrier was sitting up in it. He gave a welcoming bark as the man bent down to give him a pat.

"His owner kept him tied up all day on a short leash," he said. "No food, no water, and I bet he'd been kicked, too. He had a couple of broken ribs as well as the damaged eye. Fortunately, one of the neighbors called us about it."

Neil stared at Nicky. He couldn't believe that he was looking at the same dog. The Airedale only had one eye, but it was bright and lively. His short, wiry coat gleamed with health.

"Hi, boy!" Neil dropped Jake's and Molly's leashes while he bent down to pet Nicky and give him a dog treat. Nicky crunched it up eagerly.

The SPCA man laughed. "You'd think I didn't feed him!"

"He's great!" Neil said, looking up at the man. "Have you found him a good home?"

"Well," the SPCA man scratched his head. "I got so attached to him that I decided to keep him myself. He's got a really gentle nature, in spite of the way he was treated."

"And what about his owner?" Neil asked.

"I hope they put him in prison for years and years!" Emily said indignantly.

"He was fined," the officer said. "A good heavy fine," he added as Neil opened his mouth to protest. "And he's banned from ever keeping a dog again."

"Good," Neil muttered. "He deserves it." In his opinion, being banned from keeping a dog was even *worse* than prison.

He rumpled Nicky's ears while Nicky and Jake got to know each other by touching noses. Suddenly, he heard Lucy whimpering. He looked around.

"What's the matter, girl?"

The toller puppy whined again and took a few steps toward the entrance to the tent. Neil sprang to his feet, suddenly realizing what was wrong.

"Molly!" he exclaimed. "Where's Molly?"

He gazed wildly around the tent. People were coming in and out, and looking at the display screens. Several had dogs with them, but none of the dogs was Molly.

Molly had disappeared.

CHAPTER SIX

"Oh, no!" said Emily. "Neil, we've got to find her! Kerry will never forgive us."

Neil took a deep breath, trying not to panic. "Lucy," he said. "Lucy, where's Molly? Find her, girl, find her!"

Lucy ran toward the entrance of the tent, where she stopped and looked back alertly.

"Good girl! Find Molly!" Neil encouraged her.

Lucy bounded out into the open air and shot straight through the legs of the passersby, barking loudly. Neil and Emily were hard on her heels.

"There!" Emily cried.

Neil had spotted Molly at the same moment. A surge of relief washed over him. The shaggy little dog was wandering back and forth, trailing her leash and looking lost.

When Lucy reached her, Molly let out a bark, as if she was relieved as well. The two dogs rolled over playfully together.

Neil waited until they had finished saying hello to each other, then bent down to look Molly over and make sure that she was OK. Molly panted, bright-eyed, as if she was laughing at him for being so worried.

Neil noticed immediately that the buckle on her collar was undone. It could have come off with just a pull.

"Look at this," he said to Emily.

Emily kneeled down and inspected Molly's red leather collar. It was studded with glittery stones like her leash — just the sort of fancy collar that a pop star's dog would wear! "She couldn't have done that herself," she said.

"No," said Neil. "It was fastened when we had her, and it couldn't have come undone accidentally. You know what this means, don't you?" he added. "Somebody *is* trying to steal her."

"Well, maybe it *was* the guy in the green T-shirt," said Emily. "I can't think of why else he'd be following us around and staring at us all the time."

Neil thought she might be right. He fastened the collar again. It was quite difficult to force the end of it through the buckle when Molly was wriggling and trying to lick him. Bob, Carole, and Sarah came up with Jake just as he got it fixed.

"Everything OK?" Bob asked.

"You'll have to keep an eye on her," Carole said. "She's not as well trained as Jake."

"Maybe not," said Neil. "But this wasn't Molly's fault. I think somebody tried to take her while we were all busy looking at Nicky. Her collar was undone."

"But why take the collar off?" Emily asked.

"Look at it!" said Neil. "A dog with a collar like that must be pretty special, and with it on most people would know her as Kerry Kirby's dog. I bet the thief was taking the collar off so that Molly wouldn't be so noticeable. Then we came out and interrupted, so they let Molly go and took off."

"Just think," said Emily, "if it wasn't for Lucy, we might have been too late!" She kneeled down beside the young Toller and stroked her admiringly. "You're such a smart pup, Lucy. You saved Molly!"

While Emily was petting Lucy, Neil straightened up and scanned the crowds nearby. Plenty of people could have tried to steal Molly. There was the shifty-looking man in the green T-shirt — he was right at the top of Neil's list of suspects. Or there was the pushy photographer who wanted to take her picture. And what about the two girl fans who couldn't get enough of her? Neil sighed. He didn't see any of them in the crowds.

"We'll have to be really careful now," said Emily. "And warn Kerry that we think there's a thief on the prowl."

"Right," said Neil seriously. Then he had a thought and started to grin. "Maybe she'll be so grateful to Lucy for saving Molly that she'll offer her a home!"

Carole bought veggie burgers from a stall for lunch, and Bob had brought bottled water and bowls in his backpack for the dogs, so there was no need to go back to the barge. *It's just as well*, Neil thought, *because Rachel will be looking for Molly*. It was already time for Kerry's rehearsal to finish. He kept an eye out for her assistant as he and Emily strolled around the booths again, munching their burgers.

Suddenly, Emily gave him a sharp poke in the ribs. "Look!" She was pointing to a nearby booth with a banner that read *Whitewood Animal Rescue*. A man and a woman were sitting behind it, eating sandwiches and drinking tea from a thermos. With them were the twin fans with the All Spice T-shirts.

Hastily, Neil shoved the last of his burger into his mouth. "Let's go!" he mumbled.

When they reached the booth, the two girls said hello to them and fixed adoring eyes on Molly.

"You're so lucky!" one of them said shyly.

"Just imagine actually looking after Molly!" said the other. "Is Kerry a friend of yours?"

"Sort of," said Neil. "Our mom and dad run a boarding kennel, and Molly stayed with us for a week once."

"A whole week!" said the first twin.

Neil had already noticed two other dogs lying in the shade behind the booth. One was a beautiful blue roan spaniel, and the other was a cheerful-looking mongrel with a brown coat and floppy ears. As Jake went up to give them a curious sniff, Neil asked, "Are these yours?"

"No," said the first twin. "We're just looking after them."

Her sister pointed to a sign on the booth's wall: LET US WATCH YOUR DOG — £2.00 PER HOUR. "We're doing it to raise funds for the Whitewood Animal Rescue Center," she explained. "Mom and Dad are volunteers. They help every weekend."

"We run a rescue center, too," said Emily.

Neil was starting to like the twins. Anyone who supported animal rescue couldn't be all bad. "I'm Neil and this is Emily," he said. "We're here on vacation, on a barge."

"I'm Rosie Anderson," said the first twin.

"And I'm Alice," said her sister.

Neil wondered whether anyone could tell the twins apart. They looked exactly alike to him, except that Alice was slightly taller. He thought she was the one who had dared speak to Kerry earlier, and she seemed more outgoing than her sister.

"Do you want to officially meet Molly?" Emily asked.

The twins exchanged delighted grins and came around to the front of the booth to sit on the grass and pet Molly. The terrier reveled in all the attention, and scrambled excitedly from one twin to the other, licking their faces while her tail wagged. Lucy sat close by, as if she couldn't bear to be separated from her new friend.

"She's sweet!" said Alice.

"We saw you earlier," Neil said. He didn't really suspect the twins of trying to steal Molly, but he had to find out where they had been when she disappeared, just to make sure. "You talked to Kerry by the stage, and then you were following us."

Both twins turned pink with embarrassment. Then Alice giggled. "We saw you with that photographer," she said. "She was really funny!"

"Yeah, she's a real riot," Neil agreed.

"But then Mom and Dad said we had to help watch the booth," Rose added. "So we had to come back here. I'm sorry if we were bothering you."

"You weren't," Emily said kindly.

Neil felt relieved. If the twins had come back to the booth just after the incident with the photographer, they definitely couldn't have been in the SCPA tent when Molly went missing.

While Rosie and Alice were playing with Molly, Jake had settled down in the cool, shady spot with the spaniel and the mongrel. Lucy stayed close to Molly. *It is almost as if Lucy knows that Molly needs someone to guard her*, thought Neil.

The twins' mother, who was packing away the remains of their picnic lunch, suddenly stopped what she was doing and stared.

"Is that Lucy?" she asked.

Neil spun around. "You *know* her?"

"Yes," said Mrs. Anderson. "She's Jim Carter's dog, isn't she?"

"She *was* Jim Carter's dog. We found her stowing away on our barge," Emily explained.

"So we've been trying to find Jim," Neil said, "to see if he wants to take her back. Can you imagine anyone not wanting a great pup like that?"

Mrs. Anderson bent down to give Lucy a pat. "She's a wonderful girl. She doesn't deserve to be dumped — and it doesn't sound like the sort of thing Jim would do."

"If he doesn't want her," said Neil, "we'll look after her until we can find her a proper home."

"I saw Jim an hour or so ago," said Mr. Anderson as he handed leaflets about the animal rescue center to a couple of people who had stopped to admire Molly. "I wish I'd known — I'd have asked him about Lucy."

"You mean he's here?" Neil asked.

"Oh, yes — along with the band he works for."

"Tell us what he looks like," said Emily eagerly. "We've got to find him!"

"Well, he —"

Mr. Anderson was interrupted by a voice that said angrily, "So here you are!"

It was Rachel, hurrying across the grass toward them. *If anything, she is in a worse mood now than when we saw her earlier*, thought Neil. Once again, he couldn't help wondering what was on her mind. "Hi," he said politely.

"I've been looking everywhere for you," Rachel snapped in reply. She strode up to Neil and almost snatched Molly's leash out of his hand. "Kerry finished rehearsal half an hour ago. She wants Molly. Where in the world have you been?"

"I'm sorry," Neil began. "We didn't —"

"Don't waste any more of my time," Rachel snapped. She turned and began to lead Molly away. Molly hung back, whining and pulling toward Lucy, who stood up and trotted behind her. Neil could see that the two dogs didn't want to be separated.

"Can't you keep that creature under control?" said Rachel, tugging impatiently at Molly's leash.

"She *is* under control!" Emily said. "They're friends, that's all. They like being together."

"Well, they can't be together now." Rachel picked up Molly, who went on whining and tried to wriggle out of the woman's arms.

"I'll take her," Neil offered. "I need to talk to Kerry anyway."

"Kerry's busy," Rachel said. "Just because she let you look after the dog doesn't mean she can waste time talking to you."

Still trying to keep hold of the struggling Molly, she turned her back on Neil. Lucy let out a forlorn little bark and lay down with her nose on her paws, gazing after Rachel as she disappeared with her new friend.

CHAPTER SEVEN

"**W**hat's eating her?" Neil asked, staring after Rachel.

"Kerry's not like that! She *loves* talking to her fans," said Emily.

"Besides," said Neil, "we need to see Kerry to tell her about the thief."

"What do you mean?" Rosie asked.

Neil explained what had happened in the SPCA tent.

"That's awful!" said Alice. "Imagine if somebody kidnapped Molly!"

"They could hold her for ransom," said Emily. "Kerry loves Molly so much, she'd pay anything to get her back. That's why we need to warn her."

"We'd better go and find her now," Neil said, wishing he'd followed Rachel immediately.

"And we've still got to find Jim," Emily reminded him. "We can look for him at the same time. Mr. Anderson, can you tell us what he looks like?"

"I've got a better idea," said Alice, before her father could speak. "We know Jim. We can come with you and help you look."

"Would you?" said Emily.

"We'd like to," said Rosie. "Mom, is that OK?"

"Of course it is," said Mrs. Anderson. "I just hope you can get things straightened out for Lucy. Make sure you're back in time to pack up the booth, though."

Lucy stood wagging her tail as if she was eager to get started, while Neil went to rouse Jake from where he was dozing with the other two dogs.

"Come on, lazybones!" he said. "Time to go."

Jake sprang up immediately. Neil and Emily said good-bye to Mr. and Mrs. Anderson, and the four of them, with Jake and Lucy trotting alongside, set off across the festival grounds.

"OK," Neil said. "Now we're going to get this whole thing figured out!"

But two hours later, Neil was feeling thoroughly frustrated. He and Emily and the twins had covered almost all of the festival grounds, without success. There was no sign of Kerry Kirby, Michael Newman, or Rachel, and the twins hadn't spotted Jim. Neil and Emily used their passes to take a quick look backstage, but they had no luck there, either.

"I wish *we* could go backstage," Alice said longingly when Neil and Emily came back. "Please would you ask Kerry if we can?"

"We've got to find her first," said Emily.

"Maybe Kerry's gone to her hotel — or wherever she's staying," Neil suggested.

"She's staying on the river," Emily said, up-to-date as usual on her favorite singer's activities. "She owns a luxury yacht and she lives on it for most of the summer. It's called the *River Star*. We could try looking for it, I suppose."

"We'd better have a final check here first," said Neil. The sun was still shining and another band was playing on the main stage, but he didn't feel he could enjoy any of it while there was so much to be figured out.

Just as they were wondering where else they could search, Neil saw Bob, Carole, and Sarah crossing the field toward them.

Bob waved and Sarah ran to meet them. Her face was painted in orange-and-black stripes. She made her hands into claws and growled fiercely at Neil and Emily.

"I'm a tiger," she announced. "I'm going to eat you up!"

Emily laughed. "Tigers *never* eat their friends!" she said to her little sister.

"It's time we were getting back to the barge," Bob said as he reached Neil and the others.

"But, Dad —" Neil began to protest.

"We still have to put up your tent," said Carole. "And cook dinner. Sarah will be up much too late if we don't get moving."

"We should be getting back, too," said Alice. "Mom and Dad will kill us if we're not there to help pack up the booth."

"OK," said Neil. He knew when there was no point in arguing. "We'll leave it till tomorrow."

"Can we help?" asked Rosie.

"Sure," said Emily. "We still need you to find Jim, too."

"We'll meet you at your booth, first thing in the morning," said Neil.

With a last look around, he followed his mom and dad through the gate and down the path that led toward the bank of the bay where they had moored the *Wayfarer*. The sun was starting to go down, and the bushes growing near the bank cast long shadows over the water.

"Tent first," said Carole as they reached the *Way-farer*. "Then dinner. I hope everybody's hungry."

"Starving!" Neil and Emily chorused, while Jake and Lucy barked in agreement.

Neil and Emily got their tent from the barge and started to put it up.

"I want to help!" Sarah demanded.

"Keep an eye on the dogs, then," Neil suggested. "Make sure Jake doesn't run off with any more tent pegs. And please don't let him eat them!"

Sarah was delighted. She sat on the bank with Jake one side of her and Lucy on the other, and started singing to them.

"If I hear *'Row, row, row your boat'* one more time, I'll go nuts!" Neil muttered to Emily as he pushed a tent peg firmly into the ground.

Instead of trying to cook dinner in the *Wayfarer*'s tiny kitchen, Carole set up a picnic barbecue on the bank and started grilling hot dogs and chicken drumsticks. Bob cut up and buttered a couple of loaves of French bread, and brought out apples and chocolate. Neil fed Jake and Lucy and filled their

bowls with water, but Jake still wriggled up to him with a hopeful look when Carole served the hot dogs.

"Oh, OK, here you are," Neil said, dividing a hot dog between the two pups. "It's all right, Mom," he added, catching Carole's eye. "It's not feeding them at the table when we don't have a table, is it?"

When he couldn't even think about eating another piece of chocolate, Neil lay back on the bank. Night was falling, and the first stars were starting to appear.

This is a great week off, he thought. *When we've found a good home for Lucy, it'll be just perfect!*

Carole hauled a protesting Sarah off to bed, and Neil and Emily took the dogs for a final walk along the bank before they settled down for the night.

"Just look at her!" he said, pointing to Lucy as she nosed into all the fascinating hollows along the waterside. "She's such a great puppy — somebody's bound to want her."

"There won't be any problem finding her a new home," Emily agreed. "But it's got to be the *right* home. I just hope that Kerry Kirby will take her. She and Molly are already such good friends. And Lucy would love living on the *River Star*."

"We've got to persuade Kerry," said Neil. "It's no good just running up and asking her when she's busy. We need a plan."

"Yes!" Emily said with a beaming smile. She loved making plans. "But we've got to find Jim first," she added. "There's no point in fixing something up with Kerry if Jim wants Lucy back."

"If he wanted her, he should have looked after her in the first place," Neil muttered.

The path along the bank led them to where Askham Bay met the river. The dogs were still lively, chasing each other and investigating all the exciting smells on the waterfront. Neil and Emily followed them along the path that led upriver.

Suddenly, Lucy stopped, stood on the very edge of the bank, and barked sharply.

"What's the matter with her?" Neil asked.

Emily called to Lucy, but the young toller paid no attention. She barked again. Then Neil noticed a large white boat slowly making its way toward them.

"Look at that!" he said admiringly.

But even as he spoke, Neil began to realize that something was wrong. There was no engine noise — the boat was approaching in complete silence, like a huge white ghost. There were lights on in one of the cabins below, but the deck was in darkness.

"There's no one at the wheel!" Emily exclaimed.

Neil started to run up the towpath toward the boat. Jake and Lucy tore ahead of him, letting off a flurry of loud barks. Behind him, Neil heard Emily calling.

"Neil, it's the *River Star*! It's Kerry Kirby's boat!"

Neil pounded along the towpath, heading for a

place where the bank jutted out for a few feet into the river.

"Hey! Hey there!" he yelled. "Wake up! You're drifting!" Neil knew that unless he and Emily could do something fast, there would be an accident. Boats could be damaged, and people hurt.

Jake and Lucy stood at the water's edge, barking furiously. Then, when there was still no reply from the boat, Lucy plunged into the water and started to swim strongly toward it.

"That's right, girl!" Emily panted, catching up to Neil. "You go!"

Neil cupped his hands around his mouth and shouted at the top of his voice, "Ahoy, *River Star*! You're drifting! Ahoy!"

Lucy was still barking loudly as she swam. Suddenly, from the boat, there came an answering bark. Neil caught sight of movement by the rail of the boat, and thought he could glimpse Molly's shaggy outline. She stuck her nose through the railing and peered down at Lucy, who had reached the boat and was paddling vigorously alongside. Then, as if Lucy had warned her of the danger, Molly lifted her muzzle and howled.

"Ahoy, *River Star*!" Neil yelled again.

The door to the *River Star*'s cabin crashed open. A tall figure appeared in the doorway and dashed toward the bows.

"That's Michael Newman!" said Emily.

Neil watched as the soccer player grabbed the wheel of the *River Star*. The engine suddenly cut in. A strong purring noise came from the boat, and the water at the stern was churned up. Gradually, the bows swung around until they were pointing downstream. The *River Star* surged forward and then slowed as Michael cut the speed and brought the boat gently in toward the bank.

"Lucy! Where's Lucy?" Emily said in a panic.

For a moment, Neil couldn't see the toller. Then he spotted her head bobbing in the turbulent water of the boat's wake. She was heading for the bank. Neil and Emily ran to meet her as she splashed through the shallow water and hauled herself out.

"Lucy, you were great," said Neil. "Hey — I don't need a shower!" he sputtered as Lucy shook herself, spraying him with river water.

"Is that Neil and Emily?" Michael Newman leaped from the deck of the boat to the bank and fastened the mooring rope around the branch of a nearby tree. Molly jumped down after him and ran straight up to Lucy. "Thanks for warning us."

"We were having dinner," Kerry Kirby added. She was leaning on the rail of the *River Star*. "We didn't know we'd come adrift. Thanks a lot."

"It's Lucy you should thank," said Neil, crouching down to pass out tidbits as a reward for all three dogs. "She saw you first."

Molly barked as if in agreement. She was standing

close to Lucy, and the bigger dog bent her head to touch noses with her. Once again, Neil was struck by how well they got along, and thought what a good pair they would make if Kerry could be persuaded to take Lucy.

Michael bent down and patted the toller. "She's a great dog. Is she yours?"

"No," said Neil. "She belongs to someone called Jim."

"Lucky Jim," said Michael.

Neil exchanged a glance with Emily. His sister's eyes were sparkling. It was important for Michael to like Lucy, especially if he and Kerry really were going to get married. Neil grinned. So far, everything was going according to plan.

"We'd better get back to our mooring," Michael said. "It's funny — I tied that rope myself. I'm surprised it came loose."

Neil unwound the mooring rope from the branch and was about to hand it to Michael when he noticed that the end of the rope had been cut straight across. The fibers at the end felt sharp, as if the cut was recent.

"Look at this," he said.

Michael took the rope and examined it. "It wasn't like that earlier. Somebody cut it."

"What!" said Kerry. "Somebody cut us adrift?"

"It looks like it," said Neil. "But who would do a thing like that?"

"It's horrible!" said Emily, staring at the end of the rope as if she couldn't believe it.

Michael shrugged. "Well, no harm done. But maybe we should tell the police. What do you think, Kerry?"

"There's something else," said Neil before Kerry could reply. "We think somebody's trying to steal Molly." He explained what had happened earlier in the day, when Molly had disappeared and he had found her with her collar unfastened.

Kerry looked horrified. "We've got to do something!" she said. "If anything happened to Molly, I just couldn't bear it."

"Don't worry," said Michael. "We'll make sure she's fine."

He picked up Molly, tucked her under his arm, and pulled himself back aboard the boat. Molly wriggled and whimpered, just as she had done earlier when Rachel had taken her away from Lucy.

Neil and Emily stood watching as Michael steered the *River Star* around in a huge circle and set off slowly back to their mooring upstream. Kerry stood at the rail with Molly, waving to them until the cruiser disappeared around a bend in the river.

"This just gets weirder and weirder!" said Emily. "Do you think that the person who tried to steal Molly is the same one who cut the mooring rope?"

"I don't know." Neil's voice was grim. "There's a lot going on around here that I don't understand. But I'm determined to get to the bottom of it!"

CHAPTER EIGHT

The next morning, Neil and Emily picked up Rosie and Alice at the Whitewood Animal Rescue booth, and the four of them, with Jake and Lucy, set off across the festival grounds to continue their search for Jim.

Around the main stage, roadies were coming and going with equipment, setting up for the first band of the day.

"It's Sugar Candy first," said Emily, making a face as she studied her program. "I wonder what they're going to be like — it's their first live performance. All Spice are headlining, so they'll play last."

Neil wasn't paying much attention. He was watching Rosie and Alice as they scanned the crowds carefully for Jim.

"Let's try backstage," he suggested. "Come on, we'll see if we can get you in."

Pink with excitement, the twins followed Neil and Emily to the tent behind the main stage. A large man in blue jeans and a jacket was on duty at the entrance.

"You two are all right," he said, peering at the passes. "But I can't let you two girls in."

Neil was about to try to persuade him when Kerry Kirby appeared from the back of the tent, hurrying along with Molly on a leash.

"Kerry!" Emily called. "Can Rosie and Alice come in? Just for a minute — please!"

Kerry smiled. "Sure they can. I can't stop, though. I'm on my way to the photo shoot." She gave them a wave and dashed off, with Molly dragging at the leash and looking longingly back at Lucy.

The man at the entrance waved them all through. Rosie and Alice gazed around, wide-eyed, while Neil and Emily wondered whether any of the men fiddling with equipment or tuning instruments was Jim.

Suddenly, Lucy let out an excited bark. Before Neil could react, she took off, bounding toward the back of the tent. As Neil gave chase, followed by the others, he saw the toller puppy fling herself at one of the roadies, jumping up at him and trying to lick his face. The roadie put down the amplifier he was carrying and tried to fend her off.

"Hey!" Emily said. "That's the weird guy in the green —"

"That's Jim!" exclaimed Rosie before Emily could finish.

Neil recognized the thin, dark-haired man he had seen the day before, after the argument with the photographer. But Jim wasn't looking as happy to see Lucy as she was to see him.

"Get off, Lucy. Go on — scram!" Neil heard him say.

"What do you mean, *scram*?" asked Neil indignantly. "She's your dog!"

Jim looked startled, and stared at Neil. "Who are you? What business is it of yours?"

"We're the people who've been looking after Lucy for the last few days," Neil told him. "We found her hiding on our barge."

"After *you* abandoned her!" added Emily.

At least Jim had the decency to look ashamed of himself. "She wandered off," he said defensively. "I couldn't find her."

"Don't expect us to believe that," said Neil. "You saw us with her yesterday. You've been following us all over the place."

"I haven't been following you," said Jim.

"But you saw us with Lucy," Emily insisted. "If you'd really been looking for her, then why didn't you come and tell us?"

Jim reddened. "It's not as simple as that."

He looked down at Lucy, who was sitting at his

feet and gazing up at him with a trustful expression. Neil couldn't help feeling a little more sympathetic when he saw that Jim had gained the friendship of such a wonderful dog.

"Tell us what happened," he said.

Jim reached down to ruffle the puppy's golden fur. "I found her in the spring," he said, "hanging around the boatyard where I moored the *Green Lady*. Nobody knew who she belonged to. I thought some tourist had brought her there and dumped her."

Emily made a disgusted noise but didn't interrupt.

"I looked after her as long as I could," said Jim. "But then I got offered another job — a better job. I couldn't pass it up just for a dog, could I?"

"Why didn't you take Lucy with you?" Emily asked.

"I couldn't. The band I'm working for doesn't allow pets. And I've only got one room in London. You can't keep a dog in a studio apartment."

Neil exchanged a glance with Emily. "So what did you do?" he asked.

"Well . . ."

"You dumped her yourself, just like the tourists," Emily said accusingly. "You didn't even try to find her another home!"

"Who says I didn't try?" Jim asked.

"You didn't try very hard, did you?" said Neil. "She might have starved if we hadn't rescued her."

"Look, I'm sorry, OK?" said Jim. "I feel bad, but I can't keep her anymore. She —"

"Jim!" a voice yelled, interrupting him. Neil turned to see Dee Dee Drake coming through the entrance from the stage.

"What do you think you're doing, Jim?" she snapped as she came up to him. "Our set's scheduled to start in ten minutes. You haven't got time to stand around gossiping."

"What?" said Emily. "You're working for *her*?"

"*That's* a job worth dumping Lucy for?" asked Neil indignantly.

Dee Dee ignored all of them. "Get a move on," she ordered. "And get rid of that mangy dog. It's not yours, is it, Jim?"

Jim went even redder. He hesitated, then mumbled, "No, she's not."

"Good," said Dee Dee. "So get that amplifier up on stage *now*." She tossed her head and flounced off.

Jim stood for a minute longer looking at his feet, then shrugged and started to pick up the amplifier. Lucy got up as well, and started wagging her tail.

"No, girl," Jim said. "You can't come. I'm sorry." To Neil he added, "You see how it is."

"Sure we do," Neil replied coldly.

'You'd rather work for that horrible Dee Dee than look after Lucy," said Emily. "She's so sweet and she's still only a pup." She kneeled down and put her arms around Lucy's neck. "Don't worry, girl. We'll look after you."

Jim lifted up the amplifier and staggered off with it toward the stage.

"Hey, hang on!" Neil said. "Are you saying that you definitely don't want Lucy?"

Jim looked back over his shoulder. "I can't keep her," he said. "How can I? You heard what Dee Dee said."

"So it's all right if we find her another home?" Neil asked.

"Yes." Jim turned away, then looked back at Lucy one last time. In a softer voice, he added, "Find her someone who'll treat her right."

Neil watched him go, struggling with the weight of the amplifier. Lucy's gentle, intelligent face looked confused. She whined softly, as if she didn't understand why her owner was leaving her again, but Emily kept her arms around her and Lucy didn't try to follow.

"Sometimes I just don't understand people," said Neil.

Rosie and Alice bent down to pat Lucy, and Jake moved up to nuzzle her.

"If you can't find her a home," said Alice, "you can always leave her at Whitewood. They'll make sure that she's looked after."

"She's so gorgeous, I'm sure she'd find a new owner really quickly!" added Rosie.

"Then we'll do that, if we have to," said Neil. He grinned. "But maybe we *won't* have to. Not if I can convince Kerry that Lucy would be the ideal friend for Molly!"

There was no sign of Kerry for the rest of the day. Emily guessed that she was rehearsing for the big finale of the festival that evening, so she and Neil made good use of their time by helping Rosie and Alice with the dogs they were watching.

As the sun went down, the crowds flocked to the stage to listen to All Spice's performance. It seemed to Neil that every single person at the festival had come. Television reporters were there, and the crowd was full of people waving All Spice T-shirts and posters.

As he made his way through the crowds to the stage, with Emily, Rosie, Alice, and the dogs, Neil came to a sudden halt.

"Oh, no!" he said. "I *don't* believe it!" He clapped his hands over his face. "Em, tell me I didn't see it!"

Emily was laughing too much to answer. Neil looked up again. His mom and dad were also heading for the stage, with Sarah dancing along beside them. Bob was wearing flared jeans and a tie-dyed T-shirt, while Carole was dressed in a long patchwork skirt and a blouse draped with floaty Indian scarves and beads.

"Hi," Bob said as they joined Neil and the others. "What's the matter with you?" he added to Neil.

"I'm not with you!" said Neil. "I don't want to be seen with you looking like that."

Bob looked down at himself. "Oh, the gear. What's wrong with it?"

"It's just *so* embarrassing!" said Emily.

"It was all the rage when we were kids," said Carole. "You know — Flower Power."

"Flower Power!" Neil snorted. He plunged into the crowd again, making for the stage. *I just hope they never wear those clothes in Compton, where my*

friends might see them, he thought as he found a space at the front. *I'd never hear the end of it*!

It seemed like a long time before bright lights flooded over the stage and Kerry Kirby appeared with the rest of the band. Kerry ran to the front of the stage, waving and calling out a greeting to the audience. She was dressed in a long silver gown that glittered under the stage lights.

"She's so cool!" Emily sighed into Neil's ear as the audience clapped along.

"Hi there, everyone!" Kerry said when the applause had died down. "It's really great to see you all here tonight. In just a little while, I've got some fantastic news that you'll all want to hear, but before that we're going to play you our latest song."

"What does she mean, fantastic news?" Neil asked as Kerry played the first few chords on her guitar.

"I don't know," said Emily. "Maybe she really is going to marry Michael Newman at last. Shhh, I want to listen."

But before the song could get under way, there was a disturbance near the steps that led up to the stage. Neil could hear raised voices from the crowd. Kerry and the band stopped playing.

"Hey, what's the problem?" Kerry called out.

No one answered her, but a second later a tall figure hurried up the steps and crossed the stage to Kerry.

"It's Michael," said Neil. "What does he want?"

The crowd gave a cheer at the soccer star's unexpected appearance, but Neil thought he looked worried. Something must have really gone wrong for him to interrupt Kerry just as her concert was starting.

"Michael, this is not a good time . . ." Kerry started to say.

"I know, I'm sorry," Michael said. He wasn't speaking into the microphone, but it picked his voice up and broadcast it all over the festival grounds. "Kerry, you've got to hear this. Molly's missing. I've looked and I can't find her anywhere."

CHAPTER NINE

"What?" Kerry Kirby put her hands up to her face and stared wide-eyed at Michael. "Molly's missing? You can't mean that!"

"I wouldn't interrupt if I wasn't really worried," Michael said gravely.

Kerry glanced out at the audience. "I . . . I'm sorry," she said. "I've got to deal with this. Maybe I —"

"Take five, folks, OK?" Michael interrupted, raising a hand to the audience and managing a smile.

He took Kerry's arm and steered her toward the steps that led down from the stage. A murmuring sound rose from the crowd. Neil couldn't decide if they were sympathetic or annoyed that the performance was being delayed.

"Come on," he said. "If Molly's missing, we've got to do something!"

He started to shove his way through the crowd to the steps, with Emily just behind him and Rosie and Alice following. He thought he would never get there, especially since he had to make sure that Jake and Lucy didn't get kicked or stepped on.

When he reached the stairs, Kerry had come off-stage. The other girls in the band were standing close by, talking quietly to one another and looking anxious.

Michael had his arm around Kerry's shoulders. "She must be somewhere," he said soothingly. "We'll find her, don't worry."

"We've got to!" Kerry said. She was almost crying.
"I can't do the show unless I know Molly's OK."

Neil sometimes teased Emily for being such a big
fan of Kerry's, but he promised himself he would
never tease her again. Kerry was great. Even though
she was a megastar, she still put her dog before
everything else.

"Can we help?" he asked.

"Oh, Neil — you haven't seen Molly, have you?"
Kerry turned to him eagerly, but the look of hope in
her face vanished as Neil shook his head.

"But we'll help you look," said Emily. "Shouldn't
Molly be with Rachel?"

"Yes," said Kerry, looking around as if she expected
to see her personal assistant nearby. "She was looking after Molly while we rehearsed. Where is she?"

"I can't find Rachel, either," said Michael.

"But she knows I like Molly there when I'm onstage!"

"That's right," Michael said. "When you were getting into costume and makeup, I couldn't see Rachel
anywhere. I went to look for her, to make sure that
Molly was there on time, but I couldn't find her anywhere and her trailer was locked up. That's when I
really started to worry."

"Maybe she had to go somewhere," said Emily. "Are
you sure Molly isn't shut inside the trailer?"

"Sure as I can be," said Michael. "I shouted for her.

She knows my voice — if she'd been there, she would have barked."

"Someone's stolen her, I know they have!" Kerry said. Her eyes were full of tears. "Neil, you warned us . . ."

"It might be that rude photographer," Neil suggested. "She was trying to borrow Molly to take pictures."

"But they all took pictures at the photo shoot," Kerry said. "And that was the last time I saw Molly. Rachel had her then . . . Michael, we've got to find her!"

Michael hugged Kerry and tried to reassure her. Around the stage, the fans were getting impatient for the show to start. Neil could hear a slow clapping and a chant of "Ker-ry! Ker-ry!" that got louder and louder.

"What's going on?" said an unfamiliar voice, and Neil looked around to see a tall, gray-haired man wearing the badge that showed he was one of the festival organizers. "Why aren't you onstage?" he asked, sounding annoyed.

"Oh, I'm sorry . . ." Kerry really was in tears now. "My dog's missing. I can't go on until she's found —"

"Your dog?" the man interrupted, frowning. "You've got a crowd of fans out there who've all paid good money to listen to All Spice, and you tell me you can't go on because your *dog's* missing?"

"She cares about her dog!" Neil said angrily.

The man ignored him. "You've got to get out on that stage," he ordered, "or they'll rip the place apart."

Kerry just shook her head and covered her face with her hands.

"We can go on instead," said another new voice. Neil swung around to see Dee Dee Drake. Despite his concern about Molly, he couldn't help wondering what Dee Dee was doing there, waiting to listen to her rival band's set.

"We're ready," Dee Dee said, smiling at the organizer. "We can do it, if that'll help."

Oh, yes, very helpful, Neil thought. *With all the press here, and the TV cameras, and the fans. You couldn't hope for a better chance if you'd arranged it all yourself!*

Then something struck him. He stood with his mouth open, hardly listening as Dee Dee went on trying to persuade the organizer that Sugar Candy could take the place of All Spice. Dee Dee was dressed in tight, glittery trousers and a top to match, in the same electric blue as her hair. She was wearing stage makeup. The rest of her band were clustered a little way away; they were all in costume, too.

Just as they would have been, Neil realized, *if they'd known they were going to perform.*

"Yes!" Dee Dee suddenly leaped into the air, clasping her hands above her head. "Come on, girls! This is our big chance. Let's show them what Sugar Candy can do!"

She went into a huddle with her band, while the organizer went onstage to talk to the fans. He didn't look too happy — and neither did the fans. Apparently, hardly anyone had turned up to hear Sugar Candy sing earlier in the day.

"Listen," Neil said urgently to Kerry. "I think I know where Molly might be. Where is Dee Dee staying?"

Kerry looked up at him, her eyes wide with shock. "You think *Dee Dee's* got her?"

"Makes sense," said Neil. "What else is she doing here in costume with the rest of her band? She must have known that she would get the chance to perform in front of a huge audience."

Kerry swung around as if she was about to challenge Dee Dee, but she and the rest of Sugar Candy were already climbing the steps to the stage.

"She's staying in a trailer," said Michael. "Not far away from Rachel's. Come on."

Holding Kerry's hand, he led the way. Neil followed with Emily and the dogs, and Rosie and Alice tagged along behind.

Away from the stage lights, darkness was falling, and it was hard to see the path that led into the trees at the edge of the festival grounds. After about a hundred yards, the path joined a road; several trailers were parked in a field alongside it.

"That's Rachel's," Michael said as they passed it. The trailer was dark and quiet, but Neil still couldn't stop himself from going up to it and banging on the door. "Hi, Rachel! Molly!" he called.

No reply. Neil stood for a second, staring at the silent trailer in frustration, then ran to catch up with the others as they made their way to Dee Dee's trailer.

Like Rachel's, it was dark and quiet. This time Michael knocked and shouted, but again there was no reply.

After a few minutes, the soccer star gave up, shrugging. "Looks like you were wrong," he said to Neil.

"Well, Molly may not be here," said Neil, "but all the same, I bet Dee Dee knows something. Why else was she all ready to go onstage?"

"And what was she doing at your performance to begin with when she hates All Spice?" added Emily.

"She must have hidden Molly somewhere," Alice insisted.

But Neil could see that there was a flaw in his argument. If Dee Dee had stolen Molly, where was Rachel? Why hadn't she come to tell Kerry that her beloved dog was missing?

Rachel's mixed up in this somehow, he said to himself. He remembered how he and Emily had seen the assistant and Dee Dee talking together. *Maybe Rachel and Dee Dee set this up together.*

"I think we'd better go to the police," Michael said.

Kerry nodded, still sobbing, and Lucy padded up

to her and nuzzled her, almost as if she was trying to comfort the singer. Kerry stroked her golden head.

"You love Molly, too, don't you, girl?" she said. "I wish you knew where to find her."

"Have you tried your yacht?" Emily asked Michael. "Maybe Rachel got confused somehow and took her back there."

"Kerry's personal assistant isn't supposed to get confused," Michael said, sounding angry now. "But it's worth a try — and if Molly isn't there, I'm going to call the police."

Neil and the others followed Michael and Kerry back across the field and along a path that led through woodland and down to the river.

"This is just *awful!*" said Alice. "What if Kerry never finds Molly?"

"What if Molly's dead?" Rosie wailed.

"Don't even go there," said Emily. "Kerry might hear you. Anyway, I'm sure Molly's not dead. We'll find her somehow."

Neil wasn't so sure. His worries about Molly made him try to pick up speed, even though it was hard to see his way under the trees.

Suddenly, Jake gave a loud bark and darted off to the side of the path.

"No, Jake," he said. "Not rabbits now! Heel!"

Obediently, Jake came trotting back. Neil saw that he was carrying something in his jaws. He bent down. "Give!"

Jake dropped the object into Neil's outstretched hand. It was a strip of silvery material, tied into a bow. Neil tried to think where he had seen it before, and then remembered. It was exactly the same as Kerry's dress.

"Kerry!" he shouted. With the dogs bounding behind him he hurried down the path after the others. "Kerry, wait! Look at this!"

When he caught up, he held the bow out to Kerry. "Is this yours?"

Kerry grabbed the bow. "It's Molly's! She was supposed to wear it to match my dress. Where did you find it?"

"Jake found it just now, beside the path," Neil explained. "Molly must have come this way."

"Good boy!" said Rosie, bending down to give the Border collie a pat.

"Then we're on the right track!" Emily exclaimed with a huge grin.

"Let's go!" said Neil.

He took the lead, running down the path to where he could see the gleam of water through the trees. Lucy raced along in front, as if she couldn't wait any longer to be reunited with her friend.

Neil came to a halt at the riverbank, panting, and looked up and downstream. Several barges and boats were moored along the bank, but he couldn't see any sign of Michael and Kerry's boat.

He turned back as the others dashed out of the trees to join him.

"Where now?" he asked.

Kerry halted at the water's edge, staring at the river as if she couldn't believe what she was seeing. "Michael!" she exclaimed. "The *River Star*'s gone!"

"What?" said Neil. "Gone where?"

"I don't know. That's our mooring." Kerry pointed to an empty space a few feet farther down the bank.

Neil couldn't see any boats moving on the river, and those that were moored all looked dark and quiet. He guessed that most people were at the festival.

Then he saw a fisherman sitting on a camping stool on the bank just upstream of the place where the *River Star* should have been. Neil hurried toward him.

"Excuse me, have you seen a boat called *River Star*?" he asked.

The fisherman took his eyes off his bobbing float. "Which one would that be?" he asked.

"The big white yacht," Neil explained. "Parked — I mean moored — just over there."

He almost screamed with impatience as the fisherman turned his head slowly and examined the spot where the *River Star* had been moored.

"Yes," he said at last. "I saw her. Went off downstream . . . oh, five minutes or so ago. You've only just missed her."

"Thanks!" Neil gasped, and dashed back along the bank to relay the news to Kerry and the others.

"We've got to follow!" Emily said. "Whoever took the boat must have taken Molly as well."

"But how can we?" asked Kerry. "We haven't got a boat!"

"Our barge," said Neil. "Come on — it's not far."

They set off along the towpath, and soon came to the place where Askham Bay met the river. The Parkers' barge was moored where they had left it, near the festival grounds. Neil could see the stage lights in the distance and hear a thumping rhythm coming from the loudspeakers. Sugar Candy were well into their set.

He put Dee Dee out of his mind and turned to Michael. "This is ours. Can you handle it?"

"Sure," said Michael.

He leaped aboard, and everyone piled in after him. The engine cut in, and Michael skillfully maneuvered the *Wayfarer* away from the bank and out of the bay, into the main current of the river.

"Faster!" Neil said, desperately anxious now that they were on the move.

"There's a speed limit," Michael reminded him.

"I know, but. . . ." Neil doubted that the person who had stolen Molly and the *River Star* would worry too much about breaking a speed limit.

He gripped the side of the barge and stared at the river ahead. Jake sat at his feet, and Lucy put her paws up on the gunwale, as if she was trying to look for Molly, too.

Emily was standing on the other side of the barge, with Rosie and Alice squashed up beside her. They were all trying to be the first to catch a glimpse of the *River Star*.

It was Emily who called out, "There!"

As the *Wayfarer* swept around a bend, they all saw the white yacht up against the opposite bank and a female figure scrambling ashore. She glanced over her shoulder at the approaching barge, but she didn't stop. She climbed the sloping bank and disappeared into the trees.

"That's Rachel!" Neil shouted. "Get after her — she must have Molly!"

"But what does she think she's doing?" Kerry asked, bewildered. "I don't understand."

"I don't, either," said Neil. "But she's in this up to her neck."

Michael started to steer for the bank, but before he reached it Lucy let out a flurry of excited barks, heaved herself over the side of the barge, and plunged into the river.

"Lucy!" Emily cried.

The toller resurfaced and began swimming strongly toward the yacht. She managed to keep on barking as she swam. Then Neil heard a faint bark in reply coming from the *River Star*.

Kerry clutched at Michael's arm. "That's Molly — she's still on board!"

Rachel had not tied up the *River Star*, and the boat began to drift out into the center of the river. Michael changed course to bring the *Wayfarer* alongside it. He overtook Lucy, who was still heading in the direction of her friend's barks.

Suddenly, Rosie shrieked, "Be careful! You'll crush her between the boats!"

Before Michael could react, she leaned out over the side of the barge, trying to push it away from the yacht to leave space for Lucy, who was swimming below.

The barge swung out again. Rosie missed the side of the yacht and lost her balance. Neil hurled himself across the deck toward her, but he couldn't get to her before she tipped headfirst into the water. Wild splashing came from below.

"Do something!" Alice cried. "Rosie can't swim!"

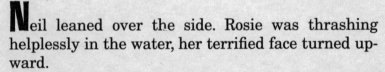

CHAPTER TEN

Neil leaned over the side. Rosie was thrashing helplessly in the water, her terrified face turned upward.

"Help! Help!" she cried.

Just as she was going under, Lucy came paddling up to her and seized the neck of her T-shirt in her jaws. Rosie grabbed at her in a panic, and the two of them floundered together in the heaving water between the two boats.

Neil was pulling off his sneakers when Michael Newman shot past him in a running dive over the side. He hit the water and came up beside Rosie and her doggy rescuer.

"OK," Neil heard him say. "Take it easy. You're OK now."

Michael got a grip on Rosie and swam with her the short distance to the barge. Neil and Emily leaned over to haul her on board. She was coughing water and sobbing with fright. Michael pulled himself up, and Neil helped Lucy to scramble in after him.

Rosie huddled on the deck of the barge, and Alice and Kerry knelt down beside her, trying to comfort her.

"Lucy, that was heroic!" Neil said, running his hands through her wet fur. "You saved Rosie. You deserve a medal."

Lucy just shook herself vigorously, and then looked up at Neil and gave a commanding bark.

"OK, cool it, girl," Neil said with a grin. "We haven't forgotten Molly."

Michael had gone back to the wheel of the barge, and was maneuvering it more carefully now to bring it alongside the yacht. As soon as they were close enough, Neil climbed over the rail and boarded the *River Star*, with Emily and Lucy just behind him.

"Molly!" he shouted. "Molly, where are you?"

Molly started to bark in reply. Following the sound, Neil dashed through the door into the main cabin. The barking was coming from below. Neil clattered down the companionway and pushed open a door that led into a luxurious sitting room.

Molly was standing in the middle of the floor, barking as if she would bust. As soon as the door opened, her barking changed to a joyful whining noise and she hurled herself at Lucy. The two dogs danced around and around each other, delighted to be together again.

"Steady, girl," Neil said, laughing. "You're OK now."

He picked Molly up and she covered his face with ecstatic licks. Emily stroked her shaggy brown fur, and came in for her share of licks, too.

"Hi there, Molly," she said. "Let's go and tell Kerry that you're safe."

As they came out on deck, they saw Kerry climbing across from the barge. The pop star's face broke into a delighted smile as she hugged her beloved dog. "She's safe! She's really safe!"

Molly wriggled in her arms, eyes bright with happiness.

"But what did Rachel do to you?" Kerry asked. "What was it all about?"

Molly's only reply was to swipe her tongue over her owner's ear. Kerry laughed and ran her hands over Molly's coat to make sure that she really wasn't hurt.

"I don't know how to thank you," she said to Neil and Emily. "If there's anything I can do, just let me know."

"Well, actually —" Neil began, grinning.

But he was interrupted by a shout from Michael. "Hey! You're drifting! Bring her into the bank."

Kerry dived for the controls of the *River Star* and started the engine. Michael steered the barge to the bank, and Kerry brought the yacht to safety alongside it. By the time they were moored, Alice had helped Rosie ashore. Rosie had calmed down by now, but she was soaked through and shivering.

"You must get those wet things off," Kerry said. "Come aboard the yacht, and let's see what we can find. You, too, Michael. And then . . ." she swung around and gazed back up the river toward the festival grounds, "and then I want to find Rachel and ask her what she thinks she's been doing."

*   *   *

Music was still coming from the loudspeakers as
Neil and the others arrived back at the festival, but
they could hardly hear it above the noise coming
from the crowd. Some of the fans were dancing and
trying to enjoy the music, but lots of them were
chanting, "All Spice! We want All Spice!" and waving
All Spice posters.

At the front of the stage, Dee Dee was parading
back and forth, clutching the microphone and trying
to sing. Neil wasn't impressed.

He burst out laughing. "Sugar Candy *is* pretty awful!"

"Yeah," agreed Emily, making a face.

Meanwhile, Kerry headed straight for the stage,
carrying Molly. As soon as the fans saw her, they
stood back to make room, so Neil and the others
were able to follow behind easily.

Michael Newman had changed into dry clothes,
and Kerry had given Rosie jeans and a sweatshirt in
place of her wet things. Rosie had recovered from her
accident in the river, and she was in a daze of happiness at actually wearing her favorite star's clothes —
even if they were too big for her.

When Neil reached the stage, he saw that Rachel
was standing near the steps, watching Sugar Candy
with a furious expression on her face.

"Rachel!" Kerry snapped. "What do you know
about all this? What did you do to Molly?"

Rachel swung around, obviously surprised to see her boss. Her angry look changed to one of guilt.

"I haven't done anything to Molly," she said defensively.

"No? Then why wasn't she here at the right time? Why did you leave her shut up on the yacht? We saw you running away up the riverbank."

"I never meant to leave her. I panicked when I saw you coming — that's all."

"And what if we hadn't come?" Kerry tightened her arms around Molly. "What if we hadn't found her? Did you think of that?" Rachel didn't seem to know what to say next. She glanced up at the stage where Dee Dee was trying to introduce her next song.

Now that the crowd knew that Kerry was back, they were shouting louder than ever. "Get off! We want All Spice!"

Dee Dee gave up trying to make herself heard, stared out at the audience for a second, and then stamped her foot and threw down the microphone. She ran offstage and down the steps. Grabbing Rachel, she yelled, "You said they'd like us! You said we'd be a hit!"

"Hey, I set it up for you!" Rachel yelled back at her. "It's not *my* fault that you messed it up!"

"*What?*" said Kerry. She was suddenly white with anger. "Rachel, I want an explanation. And it had better be good."

Rachel pulled away from Dee Dee. "All right, I admit it," she said. "I don't have much of a choice, do I? I hid Molly because I knew you wouldn't perform if she was missing. I wanted to give Sugar Candy their big break."

"And you cut the rope on the *River Star* last night," Neil put in. "And tried to steal Molly from the SPCA tent." Everything was beginning to fall into place.

"No, I didn't. That was her," said Rachel sulkily, turning to Dee Dee with a look of dislike.

"Rachel . . . why?" Kerry asked, sounding more confused than angry now.

"Dee Dee said I could be their manager. If they'd become successful, I would have gone with them. I would have been somebody." Her voice was bitter. "I'm tired of taking orders, Kerry."

"I'm sorry, Rachel," Kerry said. "I never meant to —"

"Huh!" Dee Dee interrupted. "You think you're so fabulous, Kerry Kirby. You think —"

"She *is* fabulous." Emily loyally stuck up for her favorite star.

Dee Dee ignored her. "You never gave me a chance when I was in All Spice," she said to Kerry. "You always had to be the big name, the big star. I wanted to show everybody that I could be just as good as you."

"Didn't work, though, did it?" said Neil.

"I'm sorry, Dee Dee," Kerry said, and she sounded as if she meant it. "I never wanted you to leave All

Spice, but I couldn't let you be a lead singer because . . . well, to be honest, Dee Dee, you haven't got
what it takes."

For a minute, Neil thought Dee Dee might slap
Kerry. Michael obviously thought so, too, because he
took a step forward and put an arm around Kerry's
shoulders. Molly let out a growl from Kerry's arms,
and Lucy pushed forward and bared her teeth at Dee
Dee.

"You wait!" Dee Dee said. "I'll show you! Just you
wait!"

She spun around and flounced off. The rest of her
band glanced uneasily at Kerry, and then trailed off
after Dee Dee. Kerry was left facing Rachel once
again.

"I'm really sorry," she said. "Look, we've got to
talk —"

"I don't want to talk," Rachel replied. "There's
nothing to say. We can't go on working together after
this. I'm really sorry. I'll save you the trouble of firing
me — I quit."

She turned her back on Kerry and walked away.

Kerry opened her mouth as if to call her back, then
hugged Molly to her and buried her face in the little
dog's golden fur. Michael tightened the arm he had
around her, and Lucy put her paws up on the singer's
knee as if she wanted to comfort her, too. Neil and
Emily looked sadly at each other. Everything was

over, the mystery was solved, but Kerry still had to face up to being betrayed by the assistant she thought of as a friend.

By now the whole crowd of fans had taken up the chant. "All Spice! All Spice!"

Kerry suddenly straightened up. "Hey, what are we waiting for?" she said. "I can't just stand here, I've got to find the band. We've got a show to do!"

Emily was clapping wildly as All Spice came to the end of yet another hit song. Beside her, Rosie and Alice were jumping up and down and waving at Kerry on the stage. Neil grinned. Kerry was pretty good, he had to admit.

"And now," Kerry said, as the applause started to die down, "I've got that news I promised you earlier. Michael. . . ."

She held out a hand, and Michael Newman climbed the steps and joined her onstage. He had Molly tucked under one arm.

"What's this?" Neil asked.

"Maybe they really *are* engaged," said Emily hopefully.

Kerry took hold of Michael's hand. "I know you've all been waiting to hear whether Michael and I are going to get engaged. Well, now I can tell you. We're not."

There was a murmur of disappointment from the crowd. Kerry looked at Michael with sparkling eyes.

"We're not engaged," she went on. "We're married. We —"

Whatever she meant to say was lost as the audience erupted into cheering. Michael and Kerry stood side by side, both with broad smiles, until their fans had finished showing how delighted they were.

"Married!" Emily exclaimed. "So they'll have their honeymoon on the *River Star*. Oh, that's so romantic!"

When Kerry could make herself heard again, she said, "We wanted a really quiet wedding, so we didn't tell anybody. We just sneaked off one morning and did it!"

Neil laughed. "And even that pushy photographer didn't know!" he whispered to Emily.

"You've been a great audience," Kerry went on, "and in just a minute, we've got one last song for you. But before that I want to tell you what happened earlier. As you all know, Molly disappeared." She reached out to stroke the shaggy dog. "I couldn't sing until I was sure she was all right, because Molly means more to me than anything."

"Except me," Michael put in.

"Yeah, sure, except you," said Kerry, laughing. "And there are a couple of special people and special dogs I want to thank, because without them I might never have gotten Molly back at all. Neil, Emily. . . ."

She beckoned to them to join her on the stage.

"I can't!" gasped Emily, blushing furiously.

"Sure you can," said Neil, giving her a shove toward the stage. "Come on, Jake. And you, Lucy. Everybody's waiting."

Lucy was first up the steps, and bounded across the stage to Kerry and Michael, her white-tipped tail waving ecstatically. Neil remembered how much she'd enjoyed being onstage earlier. Michael put Molly down, and the two dogs nosed up to each other in a friendly way. The audience laughed. Kerry told them all the story of the search for Molly and the race to catch the yacht. Neil noticed that she didn't mention Rachel. But she thanked Alice and Rosie, too.

"So that's how I got Molly back, safe and sound," Kerry finished. She gave Emily a hug and shook Neil's hand. "C'mon everybody," she said to the audience. "Let's hear it for Neil and Emily!"

Neil felt himself blush just like Emily as the audience clapped. He caught sight of his mom and dad in the front row, and Sarah jumping up and down with excitement.

"Kerry," he said, "it wasn't really me and Emily who saved Molly. It was Lucy. She knew that Molly was on board the *River Star*. If she hadn't, we might still be looking."

"That's true," said Kerry, looking at Lucy and smiling. "She's certainly a smart dog."

"And she and Molly get along really well," said Neil. "You can see they do."

Lucy had settled down on the stage, and Molly was snuggled up beside her. Neil knew that it would be a real heartbreak for both dogs if they had to be separated. The audience could see it, too, and Neil had to raise his voice above their murmurs of sympathy and admiration.

"Lucy's owner can't look after her anymore," he went on, "so I thought it would be a great idea if you kept her, as a friend for Molly. You've said yourself that Molly gets lonely sometimes."

"Well . . ." Kerry glanced at Michael, "what do you think?"

Before Michael could reply, somebody in the audience shouted, "Go for it, Kerry!"

Michael shrugged, but there was a twinkle in his eyes. "You can't argue with your fans, Kerry," he said. "I agree. Let's go for it!"

The audience started to cheer again. Neil spotted Alice and Rosie jumping up and down with excitement. Kerry kneeled down and put one arm around Lucy and one around Molly. "Hi there, Lucy," she said. "D'you want to stay with me and Molly for always? Molly, would you like that?"

Lucy lifted a paw, laid it on Kerry's knee, and looked up with trust into her eyes. Molly scrambled up with her paws on Kerry's shoulder so that she could slurp her tongue over the pop star's face.

Neil grinned at Emily. "I think we can call that a *yes*."

Carole Parker stared the engine of the *Wayfarer* and reversed the barge carefully away from the mooring. Neil gazed back at the festival grounds. It was the morning after Molly's disappearance and the exciting chase along the river. The booths were packed up now, and a few men were dismantling the fence and the gate.

"We've had a great time," he said.

Emily sighed. "Wasn't Kerry *wonderful*?"

"She was pretty good," Neil agreed. "Especially when she said that she'd look after Lucy. Now Molly won't be lonely anymore, and Lucy will have a good home. And she'll spend lots of time on the river when Kerry and Michael are living on the *River Star*."

As the *Wayfarer* turned into the river and headed upstream, Jake let out an excited bark and jumped up to rest his front paws on the side of the barge. The *River Star* was heading downstream toward them.

Michael Newman was at the wheel, with Kerry beside him. Molly and Lucy were side by side, poking their noses through the railings to sniff all the exciting smells of the river.

"Hi!" Kerry called and waved. "Have a good trip!"

"You, too!" Emily shouted back.

"And look after Lucy!" Neil added.

"We will!"

Neil kept his eyes on the dogs as the two boats passed each other.

"Kerry's yacht is so cool," said Emily. "It's even named after her — *River Star*."

"What?" said Neil. He laughed suddenly. "No — I think it's named after Lucy. She's the real river star!"